THE GOLDEN AXE

and other

Folk Tales of Compassion and Greed

Jacket design by Greg Brown, Abalone Design Group, Sausalito, California
Drawings by Kim Collette, Sebastopol, California
Typeset and layout by Regent Press, Oakland, California

Printed in USA by Malloy Lithographing

Other publications by Ruth Stotter

Little Acorns : An Introduction to Marin County Plant Lore
About Story: Writings on Story and Storytelling
California Tales (audiocassette)
Women of the West (audiocassette)
The Storyteller's Calendar

ACKNOWLEDGEMENTS

I would like to express appreciation to Clare Burch, Lucinda deLorimier, Laura Fadave, Barbara Fuller, Kate Kelly, McKay Russo, and Judy Sierra for their assistance with this manuscript. In addition, it was truly generous of storyteller and scholar John Boe to grant permission to use his magical effect with "The Gift of the Mermaid."

This is an opportunity to acknowledge my indebtedness to folklorist Herminia Q. Menez who sparked my interest in folklore, to Judy Sierra and Margared Read MacDonald, both folklorists, authors and storytellers, and to John Boe who ignited my interest in analyzing traditional oral narratives.

I am additionally grateful to Lawrence H. Stotter for his many years of listening to my stories.

TABLE OF CONTENTS

III. Summaries of Additional Texts

IV. Additional Summaries Included in Story Notes - - - - - - - - - 147

INTRODUCTION:

ABOUT TALE TYPE 480

This book was inspired by *The Tale of the Kind and Unkind Girl: AATH 480 and Related Tales,* by Warren E. Roberts. In 1953, Warren Roberts received the first Ph.D. in Folklore in the United States; his doctoral thesis was based on his research with Tale Type 480.

Although Roberts's book does not include stories, it does provide a meticulous listing of more than nine hundred variants of Tale Type 480, identifying and differentiating key motifs in variants from around the world. It is an invaluable guide for comparing the similarities and the differences in these stories. *The Golden Axe* is a compilation of story texts from around the world related to Tale Type 480.

Folklorists found that to compare similar stories it was necessary to have a numbering system to facilitate their research. Consequently, Finnish folklorist Antti Aarne (1867-1925) created a list of tale types, classifying stories with similar patterns into assigned types. Stith Thompson translated the list into English in 1928, and it was revised in 1961. This system allows scholars to identify, classify, and locate stories with similar formats.

All of the stories in *The Golden Axe* are related to Tale Type 480, also referred to as AT 480. Whether the heroes in these tales are adults or children, they are characterized by the following:

1. The heroes trust their intuition, knowing when it is time to leave home and when to return home.

2. The heroes show compassion without calculating what they will gain by it. They act as caregivers without being martyrs and in so doing demonstrate their worthiness for being helped themselves.

3. The heroes do chores willingly and carefully.

4. Supernatural creatures help the heroes, who are thus "gifted" — literally and symbolically. This conveys the message that assistance will become available for those who show themselves worthy of being helped.

5. Hunger and food are recurring themes. The characters might, for example, seek strawberries in the snow, not be fed enough, offer the little food available to strangers, or select the right eggs or farm vegetables. Providing or not providing food often represents solicitude toward strangers and attitude toward family members.

6. Mean-spirited, greedy people are punished by the same figure that is the donor for the hero or heroine. This figure becomes, like the goddess Nemesis, the expression of divine wrath, providing retribution and punishment.

The main characteristic of Tale Type 480 is the implicit test of courtesy or willingness to do unpleasant tasks. The good person successfully passes this test and is rewarded. The bad person fails and is punished. AT 480 is commonly referred to as "The Kind and Unkind Girl" or "The Spinning Women at the Well," even though the stories may have men, brothers, neighbors, a boy and girl, or even animals as the main characters. This tale type, with rare exceptions, does not end in marriage.

In AT 480, good behavior is rewarded, and bad behavior is punished with swift and just retaliation. Gems and gold are symbolic rewards for being a good person; the appearance of a donkey tail on the forehead, a dipping in pitch, receiving of a basket of snakes, or toads coming from the mouth are symbolic outward representations of cruelty and selfishness.

Many fairy tales provide a blueprint for leaving home, passing through puberty, becoming ready for marriage, or achieving individuation through an initiation rite. ("Individuation" is a Jungian term for achieving a balanced selfhood.) The stories in Tale Type 480 primarily fall into this last category, providing hope that no matter how abused and unhappy you may be, there is hope that if you have integrity and help those less fortunate, you will survive. The help (donor) may come in a variety of guises — a bird, a mermaid, dwarfs in the forest, the Virgin Mary, Mercury, King Frost, a witch — but if you are good, you will be rewarded and if you are lazy and/or cruel, you will be punished.

Tale Type 480 is referred to as "The Kind and Unkind Girl." Q2 is the number assigned for the motif "kind and unkind." You can use a Tale Type Index or a Motif Index to research additional stories on this theme. (Interestingly, many native American stories have a similar double myth motif where one character, for example, a father goes on a quest and disobeys the taboos and later, his son goes on the same journey, obeys the taboos, and is successful.)

Many similar motifs appear in these stories. For the folklorist, a motif is a plot kernel, a recurring element, which is characteristic of fairy tales. The motif may be a character, such as a witch, or an incident, such as the gathering of talking eggs.

Folklorists have numbered the primary motifs that appear in fairytales. Like tale types, motifs provide a way to compare story variants. For example, Shakespeare used one of the motifs associated with this story in his play *The Merchant of Venice.* Portia's suitors are asked to choose between a golden, silver, or lead box (motif #L220). The humblest of the three chooses the lead box and is rewarded. Each of the full texts in this book includes a list of the main motifs at the end of the story notes. *The Storyteller's Sourcebook,* by Margaret Read MacDonald, is a recommended motif guide to children's folktales.

Folk tale collector Andrew Lang said that the motifs in stories are like the glass stones in a kaleidoscope: the motifs spin and make new designs (stories). As you will see, the same story told in different cultures spins differently, reflecting cultural differences.

1

TIPS FOR TELLING STORIES

The stories in this book were collected from storytellers who *told* stories. In most cases, the published story is not written as the storyteller told it. Instead, the language has been adapted so the story will read well. Grammar may have been modified, incomplete sentences adapted, and the storyteller's dramatic use of sound effects, pauses, and repetitions eliminated. To bring these stories back to tellable form, to free them from the printed page, note the following storytelling tips and techniques.

1. <u>Dialogue</u> brings a story to life. Whenever the written text says "She asked him . . ," or "Her mother told her not to . . ," or "She wondered . . ," or "He decided . . .," see if you can say the line as if the person were talking. Underline the dialogue that is already in the story. Use different-colored pencils for different characters. Then look for places where you could add dialogue or change the text to dialogue.

For example:
Book: She wondered if it would be all right to enter the house.
Storyteller: She looked in the window. "Oh, I want to go into this house. I am hungry and tired. It may be dangerous, but nothing ventured, nothing gained."

For example:
Book: The house was all tidy and neat, and she sat down to eat her roll.
Storyteller: "Oh, at last, I have everything tidy and neat. Now I am so hungry, I will eat my roll."

When you are speaking in a character's voice, you do not have to say, "he said," "she answered," or "she replied." These make the story sound literary and memorized. Your listeners will know who is talking if you change your voice and your body stance as you speak for each character.

2. <u>Repetition and pauses</u> can be effective for building suspense or humor. Count to

five or ten in your mind when you pause. The time will seem much longer to you than it does to your audience. An additional advantage of the pause is that it breaks the vocal pattern and will add drama and vocal variety to your telling. It also gives your audience time to visualize the pictures your words are creating for them.

Examples:

Storyteller: She decided to go in (pause) to go inside (pause) to enter the house.

Storyteller: She saw cats (pause) cats on the benches (pause) cats by the hearth (pause) cats on the mantle (pause) cats in every corner of the room (pause) and (pause) cats on her lap!

3. You can sometimes show something, by gesture or facial expression that is happening in the story and eliminate the words.

For example:

Book: She went outside and began to sweep. And, lo! There were strawberries under the snow!

Storyteller: She went outside (mime using a broom and sweeping snow, then seeing something in the snow) And she found strawberries! Strawberries growing under the snow.

4. Sound effects help make a story seem as if it were happening at the time of telling, rather than long ago. In the story, look for places where you can sigh, laugh, cough, use expressions like "mmmm." clap your hands, stamp your foot, click your tongue, and so on.

5. What if you forget something as you are telling a story? Your audience will not know that you have omitted anything if you continue, without discomfort, telling the story. If the part you left out is important to the story line, fill it in. For example, you can say something like, "Oh, did I tell you he took his father's blue belt when he left his house? And that is what he used now to show the giant that he had powers." Or, "There is something you need to know. Back when he left his father's house . . . " The important thing to keep in mind is that as long as you do not appear distressed, your listeners will not care if you forget part of the story. They want to hear a good story, and you are the

link between the story and your listener's imagination.

6. Your storytelling will be more powerful if you take the time to really learn the story before you begin. The following steps will help:

Learning the Story

(1) Read the story once out loud.

(2) Close your eyes and watch the story take place. Try to see the characters and the scenery.

(3) Try to tell the story in your own words, just to yourself. Play with the characters and their voices. Use your arms to gesture. If you like the story, your enthusiasm and interest will carry you through this process.

(4) Reread to see if you have left out anything important.

(5) Check to see if your story has the following five features. (Not all stories have all five, but if your story does, it will tell well!)
   a. A good opening hook: an opening that will grab the attention of listeners so they want to know what will happen
   b. Humor
   c. Suspense
   d. Interesting characters whom the audience cares about (dialogue really helps with this)
   e. A clear-cut ending: you might want to add a formula ending. (See page 56)

(6) Tell the story once more to yourself. Have fun, and play with it as you tell it. Don't memorize.

(7) Tell it to someone else. There is nothing like practice. Retellings will make you more comfortable with your story, with how you tell it, and with relating to your audience. Storytelling is an art and a craft. But best of all, it is *fun!*

II
STORIES

1. The Golden Axe

GREECE

A woodcutter accidently dropped his axe in the river. Sadly, he sat on a tree stump, head in his hands. Without his axe, he would not be able to cut dead branches from trees, and without firewood to sell, he could not support his family.

Suddenly, Mercury appeared and asked, "Woodcutter, what is the matter?"

"I dropped my axe in the river," the woodcutter answered.

To his surprise, Mercury plunged into the water and emerged holding a golden axe. "Here is your axe."

"No," the woodcutter told him, "that is not my axe."

Mercury leapt again into the river. This time he returned with a silver axe. "Is this your axe?"

"No," the woodcutter replied.

Again, Mercury jumped into the river. This time when he emerged, he held a wooden axe, which the woodcutter recognized as his own.

"You found it. Oh, thank you!" the woodcutter exclaimed.

"Woodcutter, you may keep the other two as well," Mercury said, handing him the golden, silver, and wooden axes.

Overjoyed, the woodcutter returned home and told a neighboring woodcutter how he had accidentally dropped his axe in the river and then, how Mercury had come and given him a golden and a silver axe.

Early the next morning, this man went to the river and threw his axe into the water.

Again, Mercury appeared. The man said, "Help me. My axe has fallen in the river."

Mercury jumped into the water and returned with a golden axe. "That's mine!" the man said. "That is the axe that I lost." Before the man could say another word, Mercury walked away, carrying the golden axe over his shoulder.

And so that woodcutter had to return home without a golden axe, without a silver axe, and without even his own axe.

Story Notes:

From Aesop's fable, "Mercury and the Workmen."

It is difficult to verify the truth about the life of Aesop, the man credited with writing hundreds of Greek fables. Our first information is from Herodotus, a historian of the fifth century B.C., who wrote that Aesop was a Greek slave who had lived in the previous century and was renowned for telling fables. Plutarch wrote in the first century A.D. that Aesop had been an adviser to King Croesus in Lydia. Another biographer in the first century wrote that Aesop was a slave who won his freedom and then went to Babylon to the court of King Lycurgus, where he gained fame for his ability to solve riddles.

In the first century A.D., a popular collection of fables circulated in print. This was compiled by Phaedrus, and most of the fables in this collection were attributed to Aesop.

Today, Aesop's fables are still well known. Two examples are "The Lion and the Mouse" and "The Ant and the Grasshopper."

Note: See *The Sticky-Sticky Pine,* page 143 which also has kind and unkind woodcutters as the protagonists.

Motifs:
Q3 - moderate request rewarded, immoderate punished
Q3.1 - woodsman and the gold axe
L220 - modest request best
J2415 - foolish imitation of lucky man

2 The Miraculous Pitcher

GREECE

An old man and an old woman lived in a small cottage on the edge of a forest. They had a garden that provided them with onions, beans, peas, and cabbages, they had a cow that gave them milk, and they loved each other. And so they had everything that they needed.

Then, because of an early frost, they lost everything in the garden. And the very next day their cow died. That night, the old man and old woman had to go to bed hungry.

The next night, there was a terrible storm. The wind blew and rain pounded on their cottage roof. In the middle of the night, they were surprised to hear a knock at the door.

"Now who could be out on such a night?" they wondered, and the old man rushed to open the door. A teeny-tiny old-old woman stood there, and the man invited her in to sit by the fire.

"Oh, I am so hungry," the teeny-tiny woman said.

"We are very sorry," the old woman replied. "Our cow died, and the frost has killed everything in our garden. We have only bread crumbs and hard crusts of cheese."

"I am so hungry, even bread crumbs and hard crusts of cheese would be tasty," said the teeny woman. And so the old woman went to the cupboard. But when she opened it, the platter was filled not with bread crumbs and hard crusts of cheese but with fresh bread and a whole round wheel of cheese. Astonished, she brought the platter to the table.

"Have you anything for me to drink?" the teeny woman asked.

"We have no milk," said the old man, "we have only water."

"Please bring the pitcher," said the teeny woman. And when the old man went to pick up the pitcher, he saw it was filled with fresh milk. And no matter how many cups of milk they poured into their glasses, it remained filled to the brim.

That night, since the old man and old woman would have many nights to share their bed together they gave their bed to the teeny-tiny old woman. In the morning she went on her way.

A few weeks later a neighbor came to call. She was not a very nice woman. "Oh, you are still alive, are you! I thought when the frost killed everything in your garden and your cow died, you would surely have starved to death by now."

"Well, we would have," said the old woman, "except one stormy night a tiny old woman came. And now every day we have fresh bread, cheese, and milk!"

"Why, she came to my house, too," the neighbor said. "And I told her I do *not* feed beggars. Hmmm. If she comes back, send her down to see me."

Time passed, and one warm summer evening when the old man and old woman were sitting outside looking at the stars and the moon, they saw the teeny-tiny old woman coming up the path to their home. You can imagine how happy they were to see her. But they remembered their promise and told the woman that their neighbor had asked for her to visit her home.

Soon the neighbor heard a knocking at her door. "Now who could be disturbing me?" When she saw it was the teeny woman she said, "Oh, please come in. I have been saving bread crumbs and hard crusts of cheese for you."

"You will always have those in abundance," the teeny woman replied, as she turned and walked away. And from that day, whenever the neighbor opened her cupboard there was a platter of bread crumbs and hard crusts of cheese.

Then the teeny woman went back to the old couple. "Is there anything you wish for?" she asked them.

"No," they answered, "We have our cottage and our food, and each other. We are content. "Oh there is one concern. You see, we love each other and hope never to be separated. We want to remain together always."

"I understand," said the teeny woman. "And you will be."

More time passed, and some time later, when their neighbor came to call, there was no answer. Then the neighbor noticed for the first time that in front of the door of the cottage, on the right side, there grew a tall linden tree. And growing on the left side was an alder tree. The trees were leaning toward each other, their branches interlaced and intertwined. And when the breeze blew, the leaves rustled. It was almost as if they were speaking to each other.

❧ *He who digs a grave may be making it for himself.* ❧

Swahili proverb

Story Notes:

This folk tale is a rendering of the famous story "Baucis and Philemon," which appears in *The Metamorphoses*, by the Roman poet Ovid, who lived 43 B.C.. *Metamorphoses* is a long poem filled with myths and legends in all of which transformations take place. In "Baucis and Philemon," the story begins with the couple living in a small thatched cottage, and as in the folk tale, they are asked for hospitality. The guests in Ovid's story are Jupiter and his son Mercury, whom the couple do not recognize. None the less, they offer their guests hot water to wash with, fresh herb tea, and the little food that they have. To their astonishment, their wine pitcher continues to pour wine, and no matter how much they eat, food fills their platters. They soon realize that these must be gods visiting them. In appreciation for the couple's hospitality, Jupiter changes their home to a temple. Then they all walk up a steep hill and Jupiter creates a flood that destroys their inhospitable neighbors. Baucis and Philemon become the priests and guardians of the temple, and when they are very old, they are transformed into two trees that stand next to the temple interlaced and intertwined.

If you look in a story motif guidebook (for example, Margaret Read MacDonald's *Storyteller's Sourcebook*), you will find lists of story motifs. To find other stories with an inexhaustible pitcher look up motif number D1652.5.4.

The Latin word for enemy, *hostis,* is the root for the words *hostile* and *host*. This entomology graphically illustrates the choice one has for welcoming or turning away a stranger at the door. In this story, *hospitality* is rewarded, and *inhospitality* is treated with *hostility*.

Motifs:

Q1.1 -gods (saints) in disguise reward hospitality and punish inhospitality.

Q41. - general politeness

Q45 - hospitality rewarded

D1652.1 - inexhaustible food

D1652.5.4 - inexhaustible pitcher

W158 - inhospitality

Q292 - inhospitality punished

---

3. The Twelve Months

GREECE

here was once a widow who had five children. The only work she could find was baking bread for a lady in her village who would not let her take even a crust of the bread home to feed her children. When she returned home, however, she would use the dough left on her hands to make gruel. That was all the family had to eat. Nonetheless, the children were plump as mullet while the children of the lady who employed the woman were thin as mackerels.

One day the village lady noticed this and told the widow she would have to wash her hands before she went home, as she was not to take any of the dough home with her. When the mother returned home that night, she could not make gruel, and there was nothing for her children to eat.

She said, "Children, I am going to go out to try to find food for you."

She walked and walked and was surprised to find a tent brightly lit with a twelve-candle candelabra. She saw twelve people inside, who said, "Good woman, come in and join us."

"Thank you," she said, and she went inside. The people asked why she was wandering about, and she told them her plight.

Three of the young people, dressed in light clothing, asked, "Good woman, how do you get along with the months of the year? What do you think of March and April and May?"

"I like them," she said. "The earth is covered with flowers, the fruit trees blossom, the meadows are green. I am grateful for the spring of the year."

Then three people, dressed in even lighter clothing, asked, "And what do you think of June, July, and August?"

"Ah," she answered. "The warmth of summer ripens the fruit and grains. I am grateful for the summer months."

Now three people in light woolen clothing asked, "Tell us, good woman. What do you think of the months September, October, and November?"

"Ah," she answered. "That is when we harvest the grains. The forest trees are red and orange and yellow. The full moon appears larger than ever. There is a briskness in the air. I look forward to the autumn months."

And now three people bundled up in warm clothing asked, "And what do you think of December, January, and February?"

The woman smiled. "I love the quietness of the winter months. At night snow glistens as if it were filled with tiny diamonds. And it is so cozy by our fire — we tell stories and sing songs. I love the winter months."

"Here, good woman," the people said, "take this basket home to your children."

"Oh, thank you very much." And the widow ran home wondering what she would find in the basket. Imagine her surprise to find that it was filled with gold pieces! And so she was able to buy food for her children. She could even buy her own wheat so that she could make bread to sell in the village.

The lady in the village observed this and asked the widow how her good fortune had come about. When she heard about the gift from the people in the tent, she decided to go visit them, too. She found the tent, and the people saw her and said, "Greetings, mistress. How is it you have come to visit us?"

"I am very poor," she answered, "and I have come for your help."

"Perhaps we can help you," they said, "but first we would like to know if you have a favorite month."

"Oh," she answered, "I don't think I have a favorite month. The summer months are much too hot and the winter months too cold. Everything dies in the autumn, and it rains too much in the spring. Is there anything else you want to know?"

"No," they answered. "Here, take this basket."

Happily, the woman grabbed the basket and ran home. When she opened the basket, she found that it was filled with snakes, nothing but snakes. And that was the end of that woman.

The covetous person is always in want.

Irish proverb

Story Notes:

This tale appears in many story collections. Other versions appear in the following publications: R. M. Dawkins, *Modern Greek Folktales*, ed. (Oxford Publishers, 1953); Georgios A. Megas, ed., *Folktales of Greece*, trans. Helen Colaclides (Univ. of Chicago Press, 1970), 123–127; Radost Pridham, *A Gift from the Heart: Folk Tales from Bulgaria*, ill. Pauline Baynes (Cleveland, Ohio: World, 1967), pp.100–106. In this story the girl who praises months has gold coins fall from her mouth when she talks and flowers when she smiles. Snakes, nettles, and lizards fall from the mouth of the unkind sister; Barbara Kerr Wilson, *Greek Fairy Tales* (New York and Chicago: Follett Publishers, 1966), pp.225–230; *Fa-vorite Fairy Tales Told around the World*, retold by Virginia Haviland (Boston: Little, Brown, 1985).

Variants with girl sent for violets in winter:
Beatrice Schenk De Regniers, *Little Sister and the Month Brothers*, ill. Margot Tomes (New York: Seabury, 1976); Virginia Haviland, *Favorite Fairy Tales Told in Czechoslovakia*, ill. Trina Schart Hyman (Boston: Little, Brown, 1966), pp.3–20; Barbara Sleigh, *North of Nowhere: Stories and Legends from Many Lands*, ill. Victor Ambrus (New York: Coward-McCann, 1964), pp.144–154.

ACTIVITY: See script, "Strawberries in the Snow," page 151.

Motifs:

Q2.1 - kind and unkind girls

Q2.1.4* - strawberries in the Snow subtype

Q2.1.4A* - twelve Months form

Q2.1.4Ae - woman seeking food for children meets twelve men in tent.

W12 - hospitality as a virtue

Q45 - hospitality rewarded

Z122 - time personified

Z122.3 - The twelve months

Z122.3.1 - praising the twelve months

Q111 - riches as reward

J2400 - foolish imitation

Q292 - inhospitality punished

Bulgarian version in notes includes the following motifs:

D1454.2. - treasure falls from mouth

D1454.2.1 - flowers fall from mouth

M431.2.1 - curse: reptiles fall from mouth

4. King Frost

RUSSIA

nce upon a time there was a peasant woman who had a daughter and a stepdaughter. The daughter had her own way in everything, and whatever she did was right in her mother's eyes; but the poor stepdaughter had a hard time. Let her do what she would, she was always blamed and got small thanks for all the trouble she took. Nothing she did was right; everything was wrong. If the truth were known, the girl was worth her weight in gold, she was so unselfish and good-hearted. But her stepmother did not like her.

Now this wicked shrew was determined to get rid of the girl, by fair means or foul, and kept saying to the father, "Send her away, old man; send her away so that my eyes cannot be plagued any longer by the sight of her or my ears tormented by the sound of her voice. Send her out into the fields and let the frost take care of her."

In vain did the poor father weep and implore, as he loved his daughter. But she insisted, and he dared not argue with her. So he placed his daughter in a sledge, not even daring to give her a quilt to keep her warm, and he drove her out onto the bare, open field, where he kissed her and left her.

Deserted by her father, the poor girl sat down under a fir tree at the edge of the forest and began to weep silently. Suddenly she heard a faint sound. It was King Frost springing from tree to tree and cracking his fingers as he went. When he reached the fir tree beneath which she was sitting, with a crisp crackling sound he sat beside her, and he looked at her lovely face.

"Well, maiden," he snapped out, "Do you know who I am? I am King Frost, king of the rednoses."

"All hail to you, Great King!" answered the girl in a gentle, trembling voice. "Have you come to take me?"

"Are you warm, Maiden?" he asked.

"Quite warm, King Frost," she answered, though she shivered as she spoke.

Then King Frost stooped down over the girl, and the crackling sound grew louder, and the air seemed to be full of knives and darts. Again he asked, "Maiden, are you warm?"

And though her breath was almost frozen on her lips, she whispered gently, "Quite warm, King Frost."

Then King Frost eyes sparkled, and gnashed his teeth and cracked his fingers, his the crackling, crisp sound was louder than ever, and for the last time, he asked her, "Maiden, are you still warm?"

And the poor girl was so stiff and numb that she could just gasp, "Still warm, Great King."

Her gentle, courteous words and her uncomplaining ways King Frost with blankets. touched King Frost, and he had pity on her. And so wrapped the girl up in furs, and then he covered her Next he put beside her a large box filled with beautiful jewels, and then he gave her a robe embroidered in gold and silver. She put this on and looked more lovely than ever. King Frost carried her into his sledge and put the box inside, and a team of six white horses pulled the sledge toward the girl's house.

In the meantime, the wicked stepmother was waiting at home for news of the girl's death and preparing pancakes for the funeral feast. She said to her husband, "Old man, you had better go out into the fields and find your daughter's body and bury her." Just then, the little dog under the table began to bark, saying,

"Your daughter shall live to be your delight.

Her daughter shall die this very night."

"Hold your tongue, you foolish beast!" scolded the woman. "There's a pancake for you, but you must say,

Her daughter shall have much silver and gold.

His daughter is frozen quite stiff and cold."

But the dog ate up the pancake and barked, saying,

"His daughter shall wear a crown on her head.

Her daughter shall die unwooed, unwed."

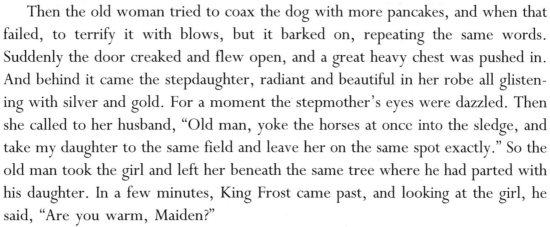

Then the old woman tried to coax the dog with more pancakes, and when that failed, to terrify it with blows, but it barked on, repeating the same words. Suddenly the door creaked and flew open, and a great heavy chest was pushed in. And behind it came the stepdaughter, radiant and beautiful in her robe all glistening with silver and gold. For a moment the stepmother's eyes were dazzled. Then she called to her husband, "Old man, yoke the horses at once into the sledge, and take my daughter to the same field and leave her on the same spot exactly." So the old man took the girl and left her beneath the same tree where he had parted with his daughter. In a few minutes, King Frost came past, and looking at the girl, he said, "Are you warm, Maiden?"

"What a blind old fool you must be to ask such a question!" the girl answered angrily. "Can't you see that my hands and feet are nearly frozen?"

Then King Frost sprang to and fro in front of her, questioning her and getting only rude words in reply, till at last he got very angry and gnashed his teeth and froze her to death.

But in the hut the girl's mother was waiting for her to return. And as she grew impatient, she said to her husband, "Get out the horses, old man, to go and fetch her home. But see that you are careful not to upset the sledge and lose the chest."

But the dog beneath the table began to bark, saying,

"Your daughter is frozen stiff and cold

And never shall have a chest full of gold."

"Don't tell such wicked lies," scolded the woman. "There's a cake for you now. Say, 'Her daughter shall marry a mighty King.'"

And that moment the door flew open. The woman rushed out to meet her daughter, and as she took her frozen body into her arms, she, too, was chilled to death.

 The horse may run quickly, but it cannot escape its own tail.

Russian proverb

Story Notes:

In similar Russian tales, King Frost is replaced by a wood goblin and a bear. King Frost, in this tale, is a powerful winter being. Jack Frost in the United States is also a winter legendary character, but all we usually know about him is that he decorates the outer panes of window glass with frosty patterns. Legendary characters are often transformed when they cross geographic and linguistic borders.

Mythical characters can be powerful beings like King Frost, or they can be amusing.

An example of the latter is the "jackalope," which has a jackrabbit's body and antelope's horns. You might find a picture of a jackalope on a postcard or mounted as a joke in a taxidermist's shop. A Mayan legend tells of the god who created horns for the rabbit, but when the rabbit lost those horns, he stretched his ears. According to *American Folklore: An Encyclopedia* (New York: Garland Publishing, 1996), tales of jackalopes have been collected in Central America, Mexico, and Africa.

Motifs:

Q2.1.4.C - The Jack Frost form
S322 - children abandoned (driven forth, exposed) by hostile relative
A289.1 - Jack Frost
Q40 - kindness rewarded
Q111 - riches as reward
B211.7 - dog announces heroine's return
Q280 - unkindness punished
Q411 - death as punishment

5. The Rooster and the Hen

ALBANIA

here was once an old man who had a rooster and an old woman who had a hen who laid an egg every day. The old man often asked the old woman if he could have an egg, but she would never give him one. One day the old man said, "Please give me an egg. The time will come when you will want something from me." But still the old woman said, "No, it is my hen, and the eggs are mine."

One day the old man said to his rooster, "Why don't you lay, too?"

The rooster said nothing, but he was sad as he wanted to make the old man happy. After a while, he ran off to the garden of the king and cried *Ki-kee-koo*. The king heard this and ordered his servants to bring the rooster to him. For some reason, the king took a fancy to the rooster and let him roam the palace. And so it happened that one day the rooster found the royal treasury, and he ate a great many gold coins. Then he pretended to be dead. The servants, thinking that he had died, threw him out.

The rooster immediately went back to the old man. "Hold me upside down by my feet and shake me," he told the old man. And when the old man did this, gold coins fell from the rooster's beak. Now the old man was rich.

The old woman heard about this and asked the old man for a piece of gold. He said, "When I asked you for one of your hen's eggs, you would not give it to me. I said someday you might want something from me. No, I will not give you anything."

The old woman went home and said to her hen, "If that rooster could give that old man gold pieces, why don't you lay golden eggs?"

The hen went to the rooster and asked, "What should I do?"

"Eat serpents," said the rooster. "Then ask her to hang you upside down and shake you." The hen did that, and when the old woman shook her, snakes came out. That was the end of that old woman.

As for the hen, it went to live with the old man, and he had a fresh egg every day for the rest of his life.

Where you are born is less important than how you live.

Turkish proverb

Story Notes:

The folk expression "swallow it whole" means to believe an outrageous exaggeration. In this story the hen literally does swallow the rooster's advice whole!

See "The Little Rooster and the Turkish Sultan" in *Twenty Tellable Tales: Audience Participation Stories for the Beginning Storyteller,* by Margaret Read MacDonald. This is the story of a rooster who swallows gold coins for his appreciative owner. In addition, the author, also a storyteller, provides tips to help in telling this story.

Motifs:
Q2. - kind and unkind
B461.1 - helpful cock
W10 - kindness
Q40 - kindness rewarded
D1454.2 - treasure falls from mouth
Q280 - unkindness punished
M431.2.1 - curse: reptiles fall from mouth
Q411 - death as punishment

6. The Three Little Men in the Woods

GERMANY

There was once a man who lost his wife, and a woman who lost her husband. Each had a daughter, and these girls were great friends who often played together.

One day the woman turned to the man's daughter and said, "Go and tell your father that I will marry him. And when we are married, you will wash in milk and drink wine."

The girl went straight home and told her father what the woman had said. "What should I do?" he answered. And being undecided, he said, "Daughter, take this boot to the well. It has a hole in it. If it holds water, I will marry again."

The girl poured in water, which made the leather contract and tighten so that the water stayed in the boot. When the father saw this, he accepted his fate and proposed to the widow, and they were married at once.

On the morning after the wedding, when the two girls awoke, milk was standing for the man's daughter to wash in and wine for her to drink. But for the woman's daughter there was water to wash in and water to drink.

On the second morning, there was water to wash in and water to drink for both girls.

On the third morning, there was water to wash in and water to drink for the man's daughter and for the woman's daughter there was milk to wash in and wine to drink. And that is the way it was after that. The truth was, the woman hated the man's daughter from the bottom of her heart.

One day, when the valley was covered with snow, the woman made a dress out of paper and said to the girl, "Put this on and go into the forest and fetch me a basket of strawberries!"

"But strawberries do not grow in winter," the girl told her. "The earth is frozen and snow is covering everything. It is so cold outside that you can see your breath. Why send me out in a paper dress? I will freeze."

"How dare you speak back to me? Be off. And don't show your face again until you have filled the basket with strawberries."

Then she gave the girl a hard crust of bread for her lunch, thinking, "The girl will surely perish of hunger or cold and then I won't be bothered with her anymore."

The obedient girl put on the paper dress and set out with her little basket. The ground was covered with snow, and she was very cold. When she entered the forest, she came upon a little house she had never noticed before. Peering in, she saw three little men sitting by a fire. The little girl knocked on the door, and when the little men opened it, she said, "Good day."

"Come in, come in," they said to her. "Sit by the fire. You must be very cold."

When she was seated, they said, "Give us some of your food."

"Gladly," she answered, and divided the crust of bread into four pieces. They asked her what she was doing out in the cold of winter wearing only a paper dress.

"Oh," she answered, "my mother made this dress for me. She told me not to come home without a basketful of strawberries."

"Take this broom," they told her, "and sweep away the snow from our back door." The girl, used to house work, took the broom and went outside. As soon as she was gone, the three little men consulted about what they should give this sweet and good little girl.

The first said, "She will look as pretty on the outside as she is on the inside. She will be prettier with each passing day."

The second said, "Every time she speaks, a piece of gold will fall from her mouth."

And the third said, "She will be a queen."

The girl, in the meantime, was sweeping snow away from the back door and what do you think she found under the snow? Strawberries! Juicy red ripe strawberries that showed bright red against the white snow.

"Take them," the little men said, and she happily picked strawberries, filling her basket. Then she thanked the men for their kindness, shook hands with them, and ran home.

When she told her new mother what had happened, gold fell from her mouth.

Her stepsister was filled with envy and decided that she would find this house in the forest so that she could have gold, too. But her mother said, "Oh, no, my darling, it is far too cold. You might freeze to death. Wait until it is warmer."

The girl insisted, so her mother wrapped her in a beautiful fur cloak, put mittens on her hands, warm boots on her feet, and gave her bread and butter and cakes to eat on the way.

The girl followed her sister's footsteps to the little house. She opened the door, walked right in, sat by the fire, and began to eat her bread and butter and cakes.

"Give us some," said the little men. But she said, "No, this is for me."

When she finished eating, they said, "Here is a broom. Go and sweep up by our back door."

The girl replied, "I am not your servant."

The three little men consulted about what they should do. "She will look as ugly on the outside as she is on the inside," said one. "Whenever she is angry, a toad will jump out of her mouth," said the second. And the third said, "She will live and die as she deserves."

And so the girl went home without strawberries, and as she angrily told her mother what had happened, a toad jumped out of her mouth. Everyone was quite disgusted.

Now the stepmother was more furious than ever with the other girl. She took a large pot and boiled some yarn in it. "Take this to the river. Break a hole in the ice and rinse the yarn."

The girl obeyed, and while she was wringing out the yarn, a magnificent carriage stopped, and a man asked, "My child, what in the wide world are you doing here?"

"I am rinsing out yarn. My stepmother asked me to do this."

The king, for that is who it was in the carriage, felt sorry for her. "Would you like to come with me and live in the palace? We will see to it that you are well treated."

"Most gladly," she replied. So she stepped into the carriage and rode away with the king. After some time had passed, the girl and the king fell in love, were married, and had a little son.

When the stepmother heard about this, she decided to take her daughter and go to the palace for a visit. The king and the girl welcomed them.

The next day the king was going hunting, and while the stepmother was with the queen, she and the other daughter picked her up and flung her out the window. She landed in a stream that flowed by the castle. Then the stepmother laid her daughter in the queen's bed, pulling the covers up high. When the king came home, she said, "Be quiet. Your wife is ill. She needs to rest." The king did not suspect anything, but when he came in the morning to talk to his wife, he said, "You do not look the same." Angrily, the sister began to speak, and a toad jumped out of her mouth. "That is because she is not feeling well," the old woman told him.

But that same evening the guard noticed a duck swimming in the river. And the duck spoke to him, saying, "What does the king, I pray you tell. Is he awake or sleeps he well?"

And then it said, "And the palace guests, are they asleep?"

The guard answered, "Yes, one and all they slumber deep."

Then the duck said, "And what about the baby dear?" And he answered, "Oh, it sleeps soundly, never fear."

Then the duck assumed the Queen's shape, went up to her child's room, and tucked him comfortably in his cradle. As soon as she had done this, she went back to the river and assumed the likeness of a duck. This was repeated for two nights, and on the third night the duck said to the guard, "Go and tell the king to swing his sword three times over me on the threshold."

The king decided, strange as it sounded, that he would do this. And when he did, lo and behold! There was his wife!

The king rejoiced greatly, but he decided to keep the queen in hiding until Sunday, when the baby was to be christened. After the christening, as they sat around the table, he said, "What punishment does a person deserve who drowns another?"

The wicked stepmother said, "For an evil deed like that, no better fate than to be put in a barrel lined with sharp nails and rolled down a hill."

"You have pronounced your own doom," said the king. And he ordered a barrel to be made lined with sharp nails, and in it he put the bad old woman and her daughter. The barrel rolled down the hill into the water.

As for the king and the queen and their child, they lived happily ever after!

ᔐ *What you do to others will bear fruit in you.* ᔐ

Singhalese proverb

Story Notes:

This story is called "The Three Little Men in the Woods," Tale 13 in the Grimm Brothers collection.

It is not surprising that in some variants the little girl meets the seasons and in others she meets dwarfs. See the play script, "Strawberries in the Snow" (page 151), which is based on a Russian variant. Marie Louise von Franze in *Shadow and Evil in Fairytales* (Tex: Spring Publications, 1980) points out that dwarfs function in fairy tales as nature spirits, impulses of pure nature. If you do your work right, they reward you.

In many AT 480 stories, action occurs at a well or a river. Water also plays an important role in this story. Ruth Bottigheimer, in her book, *Grimms' Bad Girls and Bold Boys* (New Haven, Conn.: Yale University Press, 1987), points out that (1) Water is used as a divining test to see if the father should remarry. (2) Water to drink and to wash with is clearly inferior to milk and wine. (3) Water brings about the girl's rescue as she is at the river washing yarn when the king sees her. (4) Water becomes the means of execution for the cruel mother and stepsister.

This story, like the well-known fairy tale *Snow White* has little men living in a hut in the forest who reward the girl's good manners and industry.

When stories cross geographic and language barriers, it is interesting to see how these borrowings are transformed. The following story is obviously a borrowing of "The Three Little Men in the Woods":

A girl is sent to pick berries in the winter, and she finds a lodge in the forest with four young men living there. (Note: whereas three is the typical number used in European folktales, most Native American tales use four.) The young men ask her to scrape snow off the roof, and she uncovers strawberries. They like her, and one brother asks her to spit, and when she does, she spits up a gold coin. Another brother then gives her shoes that will never wear out. The third gives her a dress that will never wear out, and the fourth a robe that will never wear out. When her cruel stepsister goes to the lodge, she refuses to spit, thinking the men are mocking her. She is vain and haughty, and when she leaves, she has strawberries, but when she spits, only toenails come from her mouth. The story continues with the good girl marrying and her stepmother continuing to do evil deeds, including letting her son-in-law think his children have died. "The Story of Spiola" *The Journal of American Folklore* 29 (1916), collected from the Upper Thompson Indians by James Teit.

For another borrowing, see the Chilean variant: "The Four Little Dwarfs."

Motifs:

Q2.1.4 - The Strawberries in the Snow subtype

Q2.1.4B - The Three Dwarfs form

H1023.2 - task: carrying water in a sieve [boot]

H1023.3 - heroine sent to woods to get fruit or flowers in mid-winter

H1245 - heroine given poor food for the journey, other girl, good food

F451. - dwarf/dwarves

      [prelude to Z65.1 Snow White tale type 709]

Q41 - general politeness

Q42.1.1 - child shares last loaf

Q41 - politeness rewarded

Q42 - generosity rewarded

D2145.2.2 - fruit magically grows in winter

D1454.2 - treasure falls from mouth

D1860 - heroine is made more lovely

L162 - marriage with prince or other favorable marriage

W152 - stinginess

Q276 - stinginess punished

W198 - unkindness

Q280 - unkindness punished

M431.2. - toads fall from mouth

7. Mother Holle

GERMANY

A widow had a daughter and a stepdaughter. The stepdaughter was pretty and industrious. Her daughter was ugly and lazy. The woman made the stepdaughter do all the housework, often sending her to sit by the well on the high road to spin. When the girl spun for a long time, her fingers would frequently bleed. One day the blood from her fingers fell on the spindle, so the girl decided to wash her hands in the well. However, the spindle slipped out of her hands and fell into the water. When the girl went home and told of her misfortune, her stepmother scolded her without mercy and said in rage, "As you let the spindle fall in the well, you must go and fetch it out again."

The girl went back to the well, and not knowing what to do, she jumped down into the well the same way the spindle had gone. When she stopped falling, she found herself in a beautiful meadow with the sun shining and flowers growing all around her! She walked through the meadow until she came to a baker's oven that was full of bread, and the bread called out to her, "Oh, take me out, take me out, or I will burn; I am baked enough already!" She went to the oven, and with the baker's iron tongs, she took out all the loaves, one after the other.

She walked on and came to a tree weighed down with apples. It called out to her, "Oh, shake me, shake me, my apples all are ripe!" The girl shook the tree and apples fell like rain. She shook until there were no more to fall.

She continued walking and came at last to a little house. An old woman was peeping out of it with such great teeth that the girl was terrified and about to run away when the old woman called her back. "Do not be afraid, dear child. Come and live with me, and if you do the housework, things will go well for you. You must take great pains to shake up my bed thoroughly so that the feathers fly about. It is then that it snows, for I am Mother Holle." The old woman spoke so kindly that the girl took courage, consented, and did her best to do everything to the old woman's satisfaction. She shook the bed with such a will that the feathers flew about like snowflakes, and all in all, she led a good life. She never heard a cross word, and there was boiled and roast meat every day.

She lived a long time with Mother Holle, but then she began to feel homesick. Although she was a thousand times better off than she had been at home, she had a great longing to go back. At last she said, "Mother Holle, I am homesick, and although I am contented here, I want to return to my own home."

Mother Holle answered, "As you have served me so faithfully, I will help you return." She took the girl by the hand and led her to a large door, and as she walked through the doorway, a shower of gold fell over her.

"The gold is yours, because you have been so industrious," said Mother Holle. Then she gave the girl her spindle, the very one that had been dropped in the well. When the door closed, the girl found herself back in the world, not far from her house. As she passed through the yard, the rooster cried, "*Cock-a-doodle-doo! A golden girl has come home too.*"

The girl went into the house, and as she returned covered with gold, she was well received.

She told what had happened to her, and when the mother heard how the girl had come to have such great riches, she began to wish that her ugly and idle daughter might have the same good fortune. So then this girl was sent to sit by the well and spin. She did not like to spin, so she put her hand into the thorn hedge to make it bloody and then picked up the spindle. She did not even try to wash the blood from the spindle; she just threw it into the well and jumped in after it. Like her sister, she found herself in a beautiful meadow, and she followed the same path. When she came to the baker's oven, the bread cried out, "Oh, take me out, take me out, or I will burn; I am baked enough already!" But she answered, "I have no desire to burn or dirty my hands," and went on.

Soon she came to the apple tree, who called out, "Oh, shake me, shake me, my apples are ripe!" But the girl answered, "I cannot stop to do that. Besides, suppose one of you should fall on my head," and she continued on.

When she came to Mother Holle's house, she did not feel afraid as she knew beforehand about the woman's great teeth, and so she entered into service at once. The first day she was industrious and did everything Mother Holle asked of her, because of the gold she expected; but the second day she began to be slower and the third day even lazier. She did not make Mother Holle's bed as it ought to have been made, and she did not shake the feather quilt so that the feathers would fly about. The next day, Mother Holle told her it was time for her to return home, at which she was well pleased, and thought, "Now the shower of gold is coming."

Mother Holle led her to the door, and as she passed through the doorway, a pot of pitch fell and covered her. Mother Holle said, "That is your payment for your service." So the lazy girl came home covered with pitch, and the rooster cried, "*Cock-a-doodle-doo!* A dirty girl has come home too!" And some of that pitch remained sticking to her, and never, as long as she lived, could it be got off.

A tree falls the way it leans.

Walloon proverb

Story Notes:

In Hesse, when it snows, they say, "Mother Holle is making her bed." This story is also called "Frau Hilda" and is Tale 24 in the Grimm Brothers collection.

Who is Mother Holle? She lives in the underworld, and the fact that plumping up her quilt makes snow fall in the world suggests that she is a liaison between nature and people, much like the months and dwarves in other AT 480 tales. Like Baba Yaga, the witch who the little girl visits in Russian folk tales, Mother Holle rewards and punishes.

In this story, the girls are tested on their willingness and ability to do housework. The good girl works adeptly and is rewarded; her stepsister is careless and is punished.

This shower of pitch occurs in enough folk tales that it is a story motif Q475.2: "pitch shower as punishment." Black pitch, like the title of the African tale "Black of Heart," is symbolic of a black nature.

Usually when the good person helps trees or animals, they provide a gift or protection later in the story. In this tale, however, the girl's kindness to nature serves only to demonstrate her compassion and willingness to help (motif Q2.1.2). A covert message in fairy tales is that compassion is one of the most important human qualities.

In the fifteenth to eighteenth centuries, spinning was an activity that was part of daily life. Before machines spun wool into thread, whenever there was an idle moment, yarn would be spun. By pretending to spin and to have cut her fingers spinning, the second girl demonstrates laziness and dishonesty. The first girl's virtue is rewarded with gold; the second girl returns as impoverished as her inner character denotes.

In Javanese and Indonesian variants, the girls are sisters. An alligator in some variants, a crocodile in others, asks them to care for a child. The good girl sings lullabies, and food and beauty are her reward. (See *The Brothers Grimm & Folktale,* edited by James M. McGlathery (Illinois:Univeristy of Illinois Press, 1988), p. 80.

Another recurring motif in AT 480 is an animal sounding the welcome home, as the rooster does in this tale, and the dog in "King Frost."

Every country has its own rendition of animal sounds. For example, here is what a rooster says in other languages.

Albanian: *Ki Kee Koo*
Arabic: *Ghoo Ghoor*
French: *Koh Koh Ree Koh*
German: *Kee Kee Ri Kee*
Haitian: *Ko Kee Oh Koh*
Japanese: *Koh Kay Koh Koh*
Spanish: *Kee Kee Reekee*
Chinese: *Koo Koo*

ACTIVITY: Find out how humans pronounce the sounds of a frog, sheep, and cow in other languages.

ACTIVITY: See script "Mother Holle", page 34.

Motifs:

Q2.1.2 - encounters en route subtype

Q2.1.2A - fall Into the Well Form;

Q2.1.2Aa - Mother Holle

N777.4 - spindle dropped into well leads to adventures.

F93.0.2.1. - well entrance to other world

F133.5 - other world at bottom of well

D1658.2.1. - grateful stove

D1658.1.5. - apple tree grateful for being shaken.

1610 - magic speaking objects

H935 - old woman or witch

G204 - girl in service of witch

A1135.2.1 - origin of snow. Snow from feathers or clothes of a witch

Q40 - kindness rewarded

F962 - extraordinary shower [of gold]

B211.10. - cock announces heroine's return

J2415 - foolish imitation

W111 - laziness

Q321 - laziness punished

Q280 - unkindness punished

Q475.2 - pitch shower as punishment

8. The Sparrow's Gift

JAPAN

ong ago there lived an old man and an old woman. One day the old man went to the mountains to cut firewood. He hung his lunch on the branch of a tree, and while he was working, a sparrow came along and ate it up. When the old man got ready to eat his lunch, he found the food gone, but there was the sparrow, fast asleep. He decided to take it home to be his pet, and he named it Ochon.

One day the old man left Ochon with the old woman while he went back to the mountains to cut firewood. Since it was a nice day, the old woman decided to do her washing, and so she made some rice starch. She said to the sparrow, "I am going to the river to do the washing; you watch the starch so that the neighbor's cat doesn't get into it," and off she went.

The sparrow, however, was hungry and ate the starch. When the old woman returned from the river, she saw that the starch was gone. Then she looked inside the bird's beak and saw starch stuck in its mouth. "You thief," she said. In anger, she cut out the sparrow's tongue.

When the old man returned from the mountains, he asked, "Where is Ochon?"

"I made some starch," said the old woman, "but while I was at the river, the sparrow ate it up. I got angry and cut out its tongue, and it flew away."

The old man was devastated. He had loved his little bird, and so he went off to look for it, calling out,

"Where has Ochon, Ochon gone?

Where has my tongue-cut sparrow gone?

Poor Ochon, where have you gone?"

The old man passed a man washing cows, who told him the sparrow had passed that way. The old man walked on, calling out,

"Where has Ochon, Ochon gone?

Where has my tongue-cut sparrow gone?

Poor Ochon, where have you gone?"

He passed a man washing horses, who told him the sparrow had passed that way. The old man continued on, calling out,

"Where has Ochon, Ochon gone?

Where has my tongue-cut sparrow gone?

Poor Ochon, where have you gone?"

He passed a man washing vegetables, who told him the sparrow had passed that way. And so he continued on, calling out,

"Where has Ochon, Ochon gone?

Where has my tongue-cut sparrow gone?

Poor Ochon, where have you gone?"

After a while he came to a bamboo grove. In the thickest part of the grove he found a house, so he knocked on the door. A voice called out, "Is it grandfather or grandmother?"

"I am grandfather."

"Then come right in."

The old man went in and found his sparrow. In fact, this was the sparrow's house! The sparrow brought the old man a feast, served on a beautiful lacquer tray. Then the sparrow said, "I have a gift for you. Would you like to have the heavy trunk or the light one?"

"I am getting old; I would rather have the lighter one," the old man said, and so the light trunk was put on his shoulders. "You must not open it until you get home. Then you may open it," the sparrow said.

When the old man got home, he opened the trunk and found to his and the old woman's joy that it was full of oban and koban coins.

The next day the old woman decided to find the sparrow to get some more coins. When she arrived at the sparrow's house, she knocked on the door and a voice asked, "Is it grandfather or grandmother?"

"It's grandmother."

"Come right in."

The old woman went in, but instead of on a tray, she was served on a dirty old board. Sticks were broken off the fence for her to use as chopsticks, and she was given sand instead of rice.

When she was about to leave, the sparrow said, "Grandmother, would you rather have a heavy basket or a light one?" "I will take the heavy one!" she said, thinking of all the coins that would be inside! "Do not look inside until you are home," the sparrow told her.

Do you think she waited until she was home to look in the basket? No. As soon as she was out of the bamboo grove, she peeked in. And when she did that, snakes and bees and scorpions came out and stung that greedy old woman.

🌀 *No pear falls into a shut mouth.* 🌀

Italian proverb

Story Notes:

This story is among the tales collected by Kunio Yanagita, a thirty-five-year-old inspector for the Japanese Minister of Agriculture.

Yanagita collected stories around Japan, as well as beliefs about folk deities and seasonal customs, and edited thirteen regional volumes related to folklore. His disciple, folklorist Keigo Seki, published a tale type index of Japanese folk tales and *Folktales of Japan*.

In some versions of this story, the cruel wife (or a neighbor) dies at the end, while other versions end with the experience changing her, so she becomes a kinder woman. In *Japanese Fairy Tales*, compiled by Yei Theodoras Ozaki, for example, the old woman repents of her unkind ways and by degrees becomes a good woman so that "her husband hardly knows her to be the same person, and they live free from want, thanks to the gift of the tongue-cut sparrow" (New York: A. L. Burt Company, 1908).

ACTIVITY: See script, The Sparrow's Gift, page 162.

Motifs:

Q2.1.2F - encounters en route subtype: Japanese

Q285.1.1 - punishment for cutting off bird's tongue

H1368.3 - main actor sets out in quest of lost bird

B222.5 - land of sparrows

W10 - kindness

Q40 - kindness rewarded

L210 - heroine offered choice between containers

L220 - modest choice best

Q111 - riches as reward

J2415 - foolish imitation of lucky man

Q280 - unkindness punished

Q2.1.4 - snakes in container

---

9. The Two Brothers

MICRONESIA

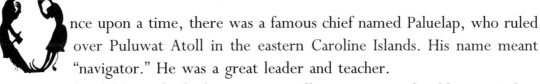 nce upon a time, there was a famous chief named Paluelap, who ruled over Puluwat Atoll in the eastern Caroline Islands. His name meant "navigator." He was a great leader and teacher.

Among the children of Paluelap were two tall, strong sons. The elder, Rongelap, was lazy and selfish. The younger, Rongerik, was a good, hardworking young man who tried to help his father. He listened to him and obeyed him.

Each son had his own home, with land, gardens, and food trees, not far from the home of their father, Chief Paluelap. They were under his rule. Paluelap tried to teach his sons, but Rongelap would never listen. It was Rongerik who learned, while Rongelap never cared to do anything that took time and work. "I'll get along very well without all that education," he said. So his father stopped teaching him.

One day, Paluelap said to Rongerik, "Now is a good time for you to learn how to make a good fish trap. You also must learn how and where to set it to get fish. At certain times of the year, it's far better than spearing."

He showed Rongerik how to cut strong reeds and weave them into a fish trap. It was a long, hard task, for the traps are large and have to be strong. Also, they have to be made in a special way, with magic words for good luck.

Rongerik listened, worked, and learned. When the trap was finished, Paluelap went out to the reef with his son and showed him how and where to fasten his fish trap among the coral rocks in the sea. They left the trap in the water for two days. When Rongerik returned, there were a hundred fine fish in the trap! He was very happy as he pulled up the trap, took home the fish, and gave his father a share of the wonderful catch.

"Good!" said the chief. "Now remember our custom. When you have a catch like this, you must share with all the men of Puluwat Island. But I do not want you to give any to your brother, Rongelap. He is lazy, and when he does catch anything he never shares it, not even with me, his old father."

So Rongerik shared with the other men. Then he set out the fish trap, and this time he waited three days before he returned to see what he had caught. There were two hundred fish! Rongerik took them to his father. "See that every family in Puluwat gets a share of them, but don't give any to Rongelap," said Paluelap.

Now Rongelap heard about his brother's fish. "Just wait and see. I'll do better than that," he said. He ordered some of his men to cut reeds for a fish trap and carried them to his father's house. He threw them down, inside, upon the floor. Nearby, Paluelap was lying on a floor mat taking a nap.

"Who's there?" he called.

"I!"

"Who?"

"I, Rongelap, your eldest son!"

"What's that you threw inside?"

"Reeds and branches. Make me a fish trap, at once!"

"I, make you a fish trap? But I'm sick today," said Paluelap.

"I don't care!" said Rongelap. "Get up now, old man, and make that fish trap. Make it better than my brother's, or I'll kill you!"

Paluelap got up, took the reeds and branches, and began to make his son a fish trap. But as he worked, he thought to himself, "Rongelap never listens to me. He knows nothing about fish traps. He isn't even watching me now so that he can learn how to make one. I'll teach him a lesson. I'll make this one like this."

Paluelap made the fish trap without a door. He knew that no fish could go into it, but Rongelap would not know that. When it was finished, Rongelap took the trap and went away.

"Rongerik, Rongerik!" he called.

"What!" replied his brother.

"Tomorrow, I'm going to set my new fish trap. When it's full of fish, I'll share with everyone in Puluwat except you. You didn't share with me!"

The next day, Rongelap went to look at his fish trap. There were no fish in it. Not far away he could see Rongerik's fish trap with so many fish that Rongerik could hardly pull it up.

Rongelap was very angry. He ran to his father's house.

"Paluelap! Paluelap!" he cried.

"What now?" asked the chief.

"What kind of a trap is that you made for me? It catches no fish. You didn't make it right. My brother's fish trap has hundreds of fish in it. I'm going to strike you dead."

The old chief said, "Is something wrong with your fish trap? Just wait for Rongerik. Maybe he will share his fish with you today."

"I don't want any fish from Rongerik!" shouted Rongelap.

Then Rongerik came along with his fish and shared them with all the other men of the island. "Shall I give Rongelap fish today?" he asked his father.

"Yes, give him some," replied the chief, "and ask him if now he would like me to teach him how to catch fish."

But Rongelap only answered, "Education is for stupid men, who need it. As for me, all I need is cleverness and luck. They are quite enough for me."

As time went on, Rongerik became a famous fisherman. He knew all the pools, rocks, and tides in the lagoon. And as he knew the best ways, the best places, and the best times for catching fish, his family and friends were never without food.

Rongelap, however, never did learn how to catch fish.

⬿ *Some are wise and some are otherwise.* ⬿

English proverb

Story Notes:

In the eastern Caroline Islands, and also in the Marshall Islands, many legends are told about the two brothers Rongerik and Rongelap. These are told in different ways in different localities, but in all of them, Rongelap is the bad brother and Rongerik is more successful.

Motifs:

L10 - main actors are two brothers (one conscientious, obedient & generous; other lazy, disobedient, & selfish)
H1550 - tests of character
H1557 - tests of obedience
W37 - conscientiousness
W31 - obedience
W11 - generosity
Q42 - generosity rewarded
W126 - disobedience
W111 - laziness
Q325 - disobedience punished
Q321 - laziness punished
L430 - arrogance repaid

10. Peesie and Beansie

PANJIB AND KASHMIR, INDIA

Once upon a time there were two sisters who lived together. The elder, Beansie, was a quarrelsome creature, apt to disagree with everybody, while Peesie, the younger, was kind and agreeable.

Now, one day, Peesie said to her sister, "Beansie, my dear! Don't you think we ought to pay a visit to our poor old father? He must be tired and lonely. It is harvest time, and he is all alone."

"I don't care if he is!" replied Beansie. "Go yourself! I'm not going to walk about in the heat."

So Peesie set off alone, and on the way she met a plum tree. "Oh, Peesie!" cried the tree, "Stop a bit. Please tidy up my thorns a little; they are scattered about so that I feel quite uncomfortable!"

"So they are, I declare!" answered Peesie, and she immediately set to work with such a will that soon the tree was as neat as a new pin.

A little further on she met a fire, which cried out, "Oh, sweet Peesie! Tidy up my hearth a bit, for I am half choked in the ashes!"

"So you are, I declare!" answered good-natured Peesie, and she cleared away the ashes. The fire crackled and flamed with pleasure.

Further on she met a pipal tree, and the tree called out, "Oh, kind Peesie! Bind up this broken branch for me, or it will die, and I will lose it!"

"Poor thing! poor thing!" cried Peesie, and tearing a strip of cloth from her veil, bound up the wounded limb carefully.

After a while she met a stream, which cried out, "Pretty Peesie! Clear away the sand and dead leaves from my mouth, for I cannot run when I am stifling!"

"Of course," said obliging Peesie. She quickly made the channel so clear and clean that the water flowed on swiftly.

She was quite tired when she arrived, at last, at her old father's house. He was so delighted to see her that it was evening before she was able to leave, and he insisted on giving her a spinning wheel, a buffalo, some brass pots, a bed, and all sorts of other things, just as if she had been a bride going to her husband. She put these things on the buffalo's back and set off homeward.

Now, as she passed the stream, she saw a web of fine cloth floating down. "Take it, Peesie, take it!" tinkled the stream, "Take it as a reward for your kindness."

So she gathered up the cloth, laid it on the buffalo, and went on her way.

By-and-by she passed the pipal tree, and lo! On the branch that she had tied up hung a string of pearls. "Take it, Peesie, I caught it from a Prince's turban. Take it as a reward for your kindness!" rustled the pipal tree.

She fastened the pearls around her throat and went on her way rejoicing.

Further on she came to the fire, burning brightly, and on it was a griddle with a nice hot sweet cake. "Take it, Peesie, take it!" crackled the fire; "I have cooked it for you to reward you for your kindness." So lucky Peesie took the nice hot cake; dividing it into two pieces, she put one piece aside to take home to her sister and ate the other as she went on her way.

Now when she reached the plum tree, the topmost branches were bending down, covered with ripe yellow fruit. "Take some, Peesie, take some!" the tree called out. "I have ripened these as a reward for your kindness."

So she picked the fruit and after eating some, set the rest aside for her sister.

When she arrived at home, instead of being pleased at her little sister's good fortune and thoughtfulness, disagreeable Beansie nearly cried with spite and envy and was so cross that poor little sweet Peesie became quite remorseful over her own luck and suggested that her sister might be equally fortunate if she went to visit her father. She told her how she had found the cloth in the stream, the pearls on the pipal tree, the cakes on the griddle, and the plums on a plum tree.

So the next morning, greedy Beansie set off to see what she could get from the old man. When she came to the plum tree, it cried out, "Oh, Beansie! Stop a bit and tidy up my thorns a little, there's a good soul!" Beansie tossed her head and replied, "A likely story! Why, I could travel three miles in the time it would take me to settle up your stupid old thorns! Do it yourself!"

And when she met the pipal tree and it asked her to tie up its broken branch, she laughed and said, "It doesn't hurt me, and I could walk three miles in the time it would take to do that. Ask somebody else!"

Then when the fire said to her, "Oh, sweet Beansie! Tidy up my hearth a bit, for I am half choked by my ashes," the unkind girl replied, "You don't suppose I am going to dawdle about helping people who won't help themselves? Not a bit of it!"

When she met the stream and it asked her to clear away the sand and the dead leaves that choked it, she replied, "Do you imagine I'm going to stop my walk? No, no! It is everyone for himself!"

At last she reached her father's house, full of determination not to go away without enough to load two buffaloes. Just as she was entering the courtyard, her brother and his wife fell upon her and whacked her most unmercifully, crying, "So this is your game, is it? Yesterday comes Peesie, while we were hard at work, and wheedles her doting old father out of his best buffalo, and goodness knows what else besides, and today you come to rob us!" With that they drove her away — hot, tired, bruised, and hungry.

"Never mind!" she thought, "I will get the web of cloth yet!"

Sure enough, when she crossed the stream, there was a web, three times as fine as Peesie's, floating close to the shore, and greedy Beansie went straight for it. Alas! The water was so deep that she was very nearly drowned, and the beautiful cloth floated right past her fingers. So all she got for her pains was a ducking.

"Never mind!" she thought. "'I'll have the string of pearls!"

She saw the pearl necklace hanging on a broken branch in the pipal tree. But when Beansie jumped to catch it, the branch fell on her head, and she fell to the ground unconscious. When she came to herself, someone else had walked off with the pearls, and she had only a bump on her head as big as an egg.

All these misfortunes had quite worn her out. She was starving with hunger and hurried on, hoping to find the griddle with a nice sweet hot cake.

Yes, there it was, smelling most deliciously, but Beansie snatched it so hastily that she burnt her fingers and dropped it. While she was blowing on her fingers and hopping about in pain, a crow carried off the cake.

"At any rate, I'll have the plums," cried miserable Beansie, setting off at a run, her mouth watering at the sight of the luscious yellow fruit on the topmost branches. She held onto a lower branch with her left hand and reached for the fruit with the right. But she couldn't reach the fruit, and the thorns scratched her. Then she held on with her right hand and tried to get the fruit with the left, but all to no avail.

Finally, she gave up and went home, bruised, wet, scratched up, and hungry, where I have no doubt her kind sister Peesie put her to bed and gave her gruel and posset.

    People aren't good unless others are made better by them.

Story Notes:

Cultural details in this story include sweet cake, the pipal tree, buffalo, posset, and a Prince's turban. It is helpful to find someone from the country or culture where a story has originated to identify objects or interpret actions. For example, the pipal or peepul tree is sacred tree of India (*Ficus religiosa*): often regarded as the reincarnation of a Braham. Many villages in India have a sacred pipal tree.

A reworked version of this story appears as "The Two Sisters" in *Fairy Tales of India*, retold by Lucia Turnbull (New York: Criterion, 1959). In this story, Tara and Hera are daughters of a Shikari hunter employed by the Rajah of Kashmir.

ACTIVITY: Write a story, telling how the prince lost his string of pearls.

Motifs:

Q2.1.2Da - The Encounters en route subtype. Two Sisters.

D1658.2.7 - a well or spring asks to be cleaned

D1658.3.3 - beings or things give the heroine a reward on her return

Q40 - kindness rewarded

J2400 - foolish imitation

Q280 - unkindness punished

Q428 - punishment: drowning

11. Humility Rewarded and Pride Punished

BENGAL, INDIA

here was once a weaver with two wives, each of whom was blessed with a daughter. The elder wife and her daughter, Shookhu, passed their time in idle amusements, while Dukhu and her mother did all the duties of the house. In course of time the weaver died, and his elder wife appropriated to herself the property he left. Dukhu and her mother were obliged to shift for themselves, and for their livelihood they spun cotton thread, made coarse cloth, and sold this in the bazaar.

One day Dukhu's mother went out, leaving some cotton to dry in the sun under the care of her daughter. A gust of wind suddenly dispersed the cotton, blowing it in every direction. As the poor girl ran after the pieces flying in the air, the wind took pity on her and said, "Dukhu, don't cry, come with me."

Dukhu followed the wind and eventually reached the door of a cow shed where she was asked by the cow standing inside to give her some food. Cows are regarded by Hindus as incarnations of their chief goddess (Durga), and Dukhu gladly did the service asked of her. She then resumed her journey, following the wind. On her way, she was requested by a plantain tree to relieve it of its overgrown boughs and the creepers round it. Again, she did as she was asked, but no sooner had she followed the wind a little further, than a horse wanted her to give it some food. She did this. Then she followed the wind again until she came to a nicely whitewashed house, which was very neat and clean inside, but situated in a very lonely place. There, in one of the rooms, sat an old lady, all alone, who was making, in the twinkling of an eye, thousands and thousands of saris. The wind introduced her to Dukhu, saying that the old lady was the moon's mother, with the world's cotton at her disposal. The girl was told to go and bathe in a river close by. No sooner had she dipped her head in the water and drawn it up again than she was turned into a surpassingly beautiful damsel, adorned with rich gems and golden ornaments. When she went back to the house, dishes of choice food were placed before her. She did not eat these. She ate only a handful of stale rice.

The moon's mother then told her to go into an adjoining room where she would find an abundant stock of the best cotton in big closed chests, and she could take any one of these big chests home with her. Dukhu did not take any of these, instead selecting a small chest that was lying on the side. The woman gave her approval. Then she said it was time for the girl to return home, and when the girl knelt, the woman blessed her.

On her way home, she met her old acquaintances the horse, the plantain tree, and the cow, and they each gave her a gift. And so she arrived home with a swift-winged colt, a necklace of precious gems, a basketful of gold mohurs, and a calf belonging to that species which gives milk as sweet as nectar.

As soon as she reached home, her mother, who had been very worried, ran forward to embrace her. But imagine the poor woman's surprise when she saw the treasures her daughter had brought back with her.

Dukhu told her mother the story of her adventures, and the latter, with a heart overflowing with joy, ran to Shookhu and her mother, recounting the good fortune that had visited Dukhu and offering to give them a portion of the wealth the girl had brought. At this the weaver's elder widow, with a long face and eyes inflamed with anger, said, "Far be it from us to take a share of what we fear may have been dishonestly acquired. I would strike my daughter in the face with the broomstick should she take a cowrie from the treasures you are so proud of."

When Dukhu and her mother retired to their sleeping room that night and Dukhu opened the chest, out stepped a prince, intended by fate to be her husband.

The next day Shookhu decided to go on the same journey as her half sister so she went outside and followed the wind. She contemptuously refused to serve the cow, the plantain tree, and the horse when they asked for her help. She was not respectful to the moon's mother. Haughtily addressing the venerable old lady, she said, "Old woman, why do you keep me waiting? Come, give me all the things that Dukhu received from you. You are foolish or you would not have given such fine things to a wretch like her. Now listen to me, or I will break your spinning wheel."

The old lady was both surprised and angry at this mode of address. She told the girl to go to the river and bathe. Dukhu had told her about her plunge in the water and becoming beautiful. So Shooku dipped herself three times in the river, so that she would be even lovelier, but when she looked at herself, she saw that her body was covered with warts. She ran back to the house, screaming at the old lady, who answered her by saying, "Don't blame me, only yourself. You dived into the river in excess. Reap the consequence of your folly."

Being then shown where the food was, the girl greedily ate the richest dishes and, after finishing the meal, insolently demanded a chest like the one Dukhu had obtained. Being told where it was to be found, she went to that room and took the largest chest. Then, without even bidding farewell to her hostess, she ran home. Everyone who saw her on her way home shunned her because of her ugly appearance. The horse gave her a kick, the plantain tree threw several bunches of its fruit on her head, and the cow goaded her. After all these humiliations, she reached home, panting for breath and half dead.

Her mother, anxiously awaiting her, fainted at the sight. The chest was, however, some consolation. Exhausted, Shookhu went right to sleep. At midnight her mother heard her cry, "Mother, I feel a torturing pain in my ankles." Her mother replied, "Child, it is nothing. Your prospective husband is putting anklets round them. Have patience, and put them on."

But Shookhu again cried out, "Mother, I feel a shivering all over my body," and again the mother replied, "Child, it is nothing. You are only being decked with ornaments." After that, her mother did not hear anything else.

Day dawned and Shookhu's mother called at her door, but there was no response. She waited two or three hours, thinking that the girl, worn out by her journey, was still asleep. But when it was nearly midday, she went inside. All that remained of Shookhu was a heap of bones, with a snake's cast-off skin beside them. The truth was evident. Shookhu had been devoured by a snake. The mother, unable to bear this misfortune, killed herself, and thus ended two lives on account of their envy, selfishness, and pride.

Dukhu and her mother, humble and virtuous, enjoyed the special gifts all through their lives.

❧ *Honey catches more flies than vinegar.* ❧

Danish proverb

Story Notes:

Note the similar motifs in this story to the other tales in this collection:

1. The moon's mother is like Mother Holle, a kind person.

2. The choosing of a large or small gift box reflects greed or humility.

3. Shookhu is reduced to bones as is the girl in the Russian tale "King Frost," page 23.

4. Snakes appear as punishment. Because many kinds of snakes are poisonous and some snakes can grow large enough to swallow a human being, they are often the villain or punishment. Note the story notes for "Anansi and His Son," page 65, another African variant with snakes.

5. The girls follow the wind. In the next story the wind carries away the girls. In the Greek myth "Psyche and Eros," the wind carries Psyche to Eros.

Motifs:

Q2.1.2H - servant girl sent to find teaspoon washed away by stream.

D1610. - magic speaking objects

G219.9 - scratching or washing a persons back that is covered

G211.1.7.2 - witch in form of cat

Q41.2 - reward for cleansing loathsome person

---

12 Black of Heart

HAUSA, AFRICA (ADAPTED)

story, a story. Let it go, let it come. A man with two wives died. When his first wife fell ill, she said to the second wife, "This illness will not leave me. There is my daughter. For the sake of Allah and the prophets look after her for me." Not long afterward, the woman died.

The second wife was left with the girl and treated her with cruelty. One day a sickness took hold of the girl and she was lying down. But the second wife said, "Get up, and go to the stream." The girl got up moaning and groaning, she was so sick, but she took a calabash and went to the stream. She filled the calabash with water and carried it home on her head. When she returned she said, "Mother, lift the calabash down for me." But the stepmother said, "Do you not see I am pounding? I'll take it down when I am finished." She finished husking the grain, and the girl said, "Mother, lift down the calabash for me." But the stepmother said, "Do you not see I am winnowing? Not now. When I have finished." The girl stood by till her stepmother had finished. Still, the woman paid no attention to her.

She said, "Mother, help me down with the water pot." Her stepmother said, "Do you not see I am pouring grain into the mortar? Not now. When I am finished pounding." The girl kept standing by till the stepmother finished pounding. Then the girl said, "Mother, help me take this down," but her stepmother said, "Do you not see I am putting porridge in the pot? When I have finished." The girl kept standing by till the stepmother had finished putting the porridge in the pot. Again, she said, "Mother, help me with this calabash."

"If I come to help you, the porridge will get burned; wait till the porridge boils." The porridge boiled, and she took it out of the water, pounded it, and squeezed it until it was finished. She did not say anything to the girl. Then, suddenly, the wind came like a whirlwind; it lifted the girl and went off with her, and her stepmother did not know where she had gone.

The wind took her deep into the bush. All alone, the girl walked and looked about, and she came upon a grass hut, so she peeped in. She saw a thighbone and a dog inside! The girl drew back, but the thighbone said, "Us, us!" and then the dog spoke, saying, "He says you are to enter." The girl entered the hut, and knelt down and prostrated herself, and the thighbone said, "Us, us!" and the dog said, "He says, Can you cook food?" And the girl said, "Yes." So they gave her one grain of rice and said she was to cook it! She picked up the single grain of rice, put it in the mortar, and pounded. Rice filled the mortar! She dry-pounded the rice and poured it from a height to let the wind blow away the chaff. Then she washed the rice, set the pot on the fire, and poured in the rice. In a short time, rice filled the pot.

Then the thighbone said, "Us, us!" and the dog said, "He wants to know if you are able to make soup?" The girl said, "Yes, I can." The dog brought the girl a very old-looking bone. She put it in the pot, and after a while, meat filled the pot!

When the meat was ready, she poured in salt and spices. When the soup was ready, she took the pot off the fire and served out the food. She divided it up, giving ten helpings to the thighbone, nine helpings to the dog, and two helpings for herself.

They went to sleep, and when it was dawn, the thighbone said, "Us! us!" The dog said to the maiden, "Can you make 'fura' cakes?" She said, "Yes." The dog brought her one grain of corn. The girl put it in the mortar, added water, and with the pestle she wet-pounded, and corn filled the mortar. Then she winnowed it, washed it, pounded it again very finely, rolled it into cakes, and put these in a pot of water. When she had finished making the fura cakes, she gave three to the thighbone, and two to the dog, and she took one. Then the thighbone said, "Us, us!" and the dog said, "He says, 'Are you ready to go home?'"

"Yes," she said, "I want to go, but I do not know the way."

Again the thighbone said, "Us, us!" and the dog left the hut and returned with slaves, cattle, sheep, horses, fowls, camels, ostriches, and robes. He said, "These are for you. They will help you on your journey." The girl thanked the dog and thighbone. Then she said, "I want to go home, but I do not know the way." So the thighbone told the dog to lead the girl back home.

When they were close to her home, the girl sent a messenger to tell the chief she was returning and wanted to enter the village. The chief and other villagers came to accompany her back to the village. When they were in the village, she took out one-tenth of her gifts and gave them to the chief. Pleased, and liking the girl, the chief asked her to visit with him. This she did, and later they were married.

When the stepmother learned of this, she was envious, so she told her own daughter to go to the steam to draw water for her. But her daughter said, "Mother, I am not going." The mother lifted a reed, and the girl went to the stream by compulsion. She drew water and took it home and said, "Mother, help me down with the pot." But her mother said, "I am pounding. Wait till I have finished." When the mother had finished the pounding, the girl said, "Mother help me take the calabash down," but her mother answered, "I am going to winnow. Wait till I have finished." When she finished winnowing, the girl asked again, "Mother, help me take the calabash down." Her mother said, "I am just going to pound. Wait till I have finished."

While she was pounding, the wind came and lifted the girl and carried her deep into the bush. Alone, walking in the bush, she suddenly saw a grass hut, so she peeped in and was surprised to see a thighbone and a dog. The thighbone said, "Us, us!" Then the dog said, "He says you are to come." So she went in and said, "Here I am." The thighbone said, "Us! us!" and then the dog said, "He says you are to sit down." So she sat down, saying, "Mercy on us, a thighbone that talks. What does 'Us, us!' mean?" But they gave no answer. Then the thighbone said, "Us, us!" and the dog said, "He says, 'Can you cook food?" And she said, "Ah, I see why you wanted me to enter. You need a cook. Ah, it's a bad year when the partridge sees them planting the seeds. I certainly hope you have grain if you expect me to be able to cook." The dog brought her one single grain of rice. "What's this? How can one single grain of rice make food?" The dog replied, "Show us how you cook." So she put the rice in the mortar and pounded it. To her surprise, the mortar was filled with rice. She dry-pounded it, poured it out so as to blow away the chaff, poured on water, and cooked. it. Then the dog brought her a very old-looking bone and asked her to make soup. She said, "Are you conjurers?" There was no answer, so she washed the bone and put it in the pot. In a short time the pot was full of meat. The girl was amazed as she stirred the food. When it was finished, she took it out and gave three servings to the thighbone, and two to the dog, and kept the rest for herself. Then they all slept. At dawn the thighbone said, "Us, us!" The dog went out and brought back blind men, lepers, blind horses, and lame asses and sheep, and then he said he would show her the way home.

When they were near the village, the girl sent one leper to tell the chief she had returned and wanted to enter the village. Remembering the last girl who had returned to the village, the chief prepared a warm welcome and was accompanied by many people when he met the girl. They walked back to the village, but by the time they reached the open space in front of the chief's house, the bad smells from the girl's retinue filled the town.

"You must go away from the village," the chief told the girl. "You must stay always at a distance from this town." When the girl's mother heard this, she became black of heart and died. That is all. Off with the rat's head.

Then the storyteller who told this story added, "This is an old story and this was the first appearance of wickedness, which is not a beautiful thing. Whoever commits a sin against another it comes back on himself. As a certain learned man said, 'Whosoever sows evil it comes forth in his own garden.' That is all. Off with the rat's head."

Story Notes:

Fura cakes are commonly made by travellers who carry flour with them and mix it with water, and sometimes sour milk.

Note the formula opening and closing used by the storyteller in this story and the next story, also from West Africa. In the United States, our typical formula openings and closings are "Once upon a time" and "They lived happily ever after." The formula opening establishes that a story is to be told. It is a marker, an indication that everyday speech has ended, now it is story time. With these few words, the listener leaves the everyday world and enters the never-never land of story. Listening to a story is different than listening to the transmission of factual content, and the listener often falls into a light, hypnotic trance state. Here are some other formula openings and closings:

OPENINGS

It was thousands of moons ago when...
Blackfoot Native American Indian
There was one time, one time there was...
Italian
Long ago in the dreamtime ...
Australian aboriginal
In a certain kingdom in a certain land in a little village there lived...
Russian
Once upon a time, a time passes, a time is coming... *Yoruba* (Nigerian)
Before the world was finished... *Navaho*
Here is a story. Let it come, let it come! ...
African
Long ago, all the sounds were music and everything was good in the world. Now, not that long ago, but in between then and now there lived .... *Irish*
Before the world became as it is today ....

Cherokee, Native American Indian

Once upon a time, and a very good time it was, too, when the streets were paved with penny loaves and houses were whitewashed with buttermilk... *Irish*

CLOSINGS

In that town there was a well, and in that well there was a bell. And that is all I have to tell. *Russian*

Mulberry, mulberry, that makes two. I've told my story, so must you. *Arabian*

It's all true, you realize. Why, I saw it with my own eyes. *French*

From then on they lived together in great prosperity and happiness. *Russian*

My story that I've told is this: let some go and let some come! *Ghana* (West African)

This is my story, which I have now told you. Whether it is sweet or whether it is not sweet, take a bit of it and keep the rest under your pillow. *Ghana* (West African)

Shimyaa. "It's finished" *Japanese*

Konde oshima. "This is the end." *Japanese*

If my story is not true, may the soles of my shoes turn to buttermilk. *Irish*

If I get another story, I'll stick it behind your ears. *Ghana* (West African)

They married and lived well, and may we live even better. *Greek*

There now is the story for you, from the first word to the last, as I heard it from my grandmother. *Irish*

Motifs:

Z115 - wind personified

W26 - patience

Q41. - general politeness

Q42.1.1 - child shares last loaf

W10 - kindness

W11 - generosity

D1610 - magic speaking objects

D1472.2 - magic food supplier

D1013 - magic bone of animal

D1658.3.1 - grateful objects give advice

B210 - speaking animals [dog]

L162- favorable marriage

Q111 - riches as reward

W152 -stinginess

Q276 - stinginess punished

Q291 - hard-heartedness punished

Q411 - death as punishment [of mother]

13. Making Stew

HAUSA, AFRICA

his is a story about Salt, Daudawa (ground millet), Nari (spice), Onion-leaves, Pepper, and Daudawar-batso (a sauce). A story, a story! Let it go; let it come.

Salt, Daudawa, Nari, Onion-leaves, Pepper, and Daudawar-batso heard a report about a beautiful youth, the son of a spirit. They decided to seek this youth, and so they turned themselves into beautiful maidens and set off. They had not gone far when they drove Daudawar-batso off, telling her she had a bad smell and they did not want to travel with her.

Daudawar-batso waited awhile, and then she followed behind.

When the others reached a stream, they came across an old woman who was bathing. She said, "Girls, rub down my back," but they said, "May Allah save us that we should lift our hands to touch an old woman's back."

Soon Daudawar-batso came and saw the old woman washing. "Good day," she greeted the old woman, and the old woman said, "Maiden, where are you going?" Daudawar-batso replied, "I am going to where a certain youth is." The old woman said, "Rub my back for me," and Daudawar-batso said, "All right." She stopped and carefully rubbed the old woman's back. The old woman said, "May Allah bless you. The youth to whom you are all going to, do you know his name?" Daudawar-batso said, "No, I do not know his name." Then the old woman said, "He is my son, his name is Daskandarini, but you must not tell anyone else." Then Daudawar-batso had to run to catch up with the others.

She followed them to the place where the boy was. They were about to enter his hut, but he said, "Go back. I want you to enter one at a time."

First Salt came forward. She was about to enter, when the boy said, "Who is there?" She said, "It is I." "Who are you?" "It is Salt, who makes the soup tasty." He said, "What is my name?" "I do not know your name, little boy, I do not know your name." Then he said, "Go back, little girl, go back." She turned back.

Next Daudawa came forward. When she was about to enter, the boy asked, "Who are you? What is your name?" "My name is Daudawa, who makes the soup sweet." And he said, "What is my name?" She said, "I do not know your name, little boy, I do not know your name." Then he said, "Go back, little girl, go back." She turned back and sat down.

Than Nari rose up and came forward, and she was about to enter when he asked, "Who is this little girl? Who is this?" She said, "It is I who greet you, little boy, it is I who greet you." "What is your name, little girl, what is your name?" "My name is Nari, who makes the soup savory." "I have heard your name, little girl, I have heard your name. Speak my name." She said, "I do not know your name, little boy, I do not know your name." "Turn back, little girl, turn back." So she turned back, and sat down.

Then Onion-leaves stuck her head into the hut, and he asked, "Who is this little girl, who is this?" "It is I who salute you little boy, it is I who salute you." "What is your name, little girl, what is your name?" "My name is Onion-leaves, who makes the soup smell nicely." He said, "I have heard your name, little girl. What is my name?" She said, "I do not know your name, little boy, I do not know your name." Then he said, "Go back, little girl, go back." She turned back.

Now Pepper came along; she said, "Your pardon, little boy, your pardon." Again, he asked who was there. She said, "It is I, Pepper, little boy, it is I, Pepper, who makes the soup hot." "I have heard your name, little girl, I have heard your name. Speak my name." She said, "I do not know your name, little boy, I do not know your name." "Turn back, little girl, turn back."

They said, "We are going back." But Daudawar-batso stepped forward and said, "Even if I do not have a good smell, can I not try to enter, too? If you were all driven away, I will be driven away too, but I would like to try to enter."

"Go ahead, try," they told her, so she got up and went to the doorway. The boy said, "Who is there, little girl, who is there?" And she said, "It is I who am greeting you, little boy, it is I who am greeting you." "What is your name, little girl, what is your name?" "My name is Batso, little boy, my name is Daudawar-batso." "He said, "I have heard your name, little girl, I have heard your name. Do you know my name?" She said, "Daskandarini, little boy, Daskandarini." And he said, "Enter."

When she was inside, a rug was spread for her, and she was given new clothes and gold slippers. She invited the others inside, and they were grateful. One said, "I will always sweep for you"; another, "I will pound for you." Another said, "I will draw water for you"; and another, "I will pound the ingredients of the soup"; and another, "I will stir the food." They all helped her.

And the storyteller who told this story added:
"And the moral of all this is, if you see a person who is poor, do not despise him. You do not know but that someday that person may be better than you. That is all. Off with the rat's head."

Story Notes:

Note the formula opening and closing used by the storyteller in this story and in "Black of Heart," another story from West Africa. This story is the original text as collected by the anthropologist. *The Golden Axe* has tried to include stories collected as close to the source as possible. As folklorist and author Richard Dorson points out, there is often a need to check African story retellings with the original texts to recognize the "charming interpretations" of the author-revisor. *(African Folklore.* New York: Anchor Books, 1972).

This story is reminiscent of riddle stories told by the Hausa and Yoruba, both West African, with many similar beliefs and values. This story may be part of a larger riddle-story complex.

Motifs:
Q2.1.2E-Encounters en route subtype: African and Afro-American tradition
see also: Q2.1.6Ba
H935-old woman or witch [name of male spirit, her son]
Q41-general politeness

14. The String of Beads

CONGO, AFRICA

wo sisters each have a string of beads made from cowrie shells, which will be their dowries. They hate their younger sister because her necklace is more valuable; it is made from coral beads. One day they secretly bury their necklaces in the mud and tell their sister that they have thrown their necklaces into the river to the water goblin, who will give them back twice as many necklaces. They persuade her to throw her coral necklace into the river, and after she does, they put theirs back on and laugh at her. Without her necklace she will never be able to marry

The youngest sister politely asks the river to return her beads. The water tells her to walk downstream. As she walks, she continues to ask the water to please return her beads. After a while she comes to a waterfall, and under the waterfall is a hut with a very ugly old woman who has many wounds. The girl strips off her own garment to bind the old woman's wounds.

A giant is heard approaching, and the old woman hides the little girl so he does not see her. Then she gives her food, and after eating, the little girl sleeps in the hut. In the morning the old woman puts a beautiful string of beads around her neck and rings of gold on her arms and ankles. Around the girl's waist she puts a kirtle of the softest and finest kidskin with copper fringe. Over her shoulders she throws a silver jackal skin. Then she gives her a magic stone to help her cross the river. When the girl reaches the opposite riverbank, she throws back the stone and continues home.

When the two sisters see this, they decide to find the old woman and ask for the same gifts. They refuse to bind up her wounds, call her jeering names, and demand the gifts. Suddenly the hut sinks from sight and the maidens find that their own necklaces are no longer around their necks. They turn to return home and are forced to run from the giant, who pelts them with stones, while the wind howls and rain sweeps through the trees. Without their necklaces, it is likely that they will never wed.

Pretty is as pretty does

U.S. proverb

Story Notes:

A variant of this tale is told by Lauren van der Post and appears in *Kaleidoscope* by Helen Luke (New York: Parabola Books, 1992), pp. 207-209.

Here is another variant from West Africa, in which two brothers are the main characters. The younger brother lets a strange fish caught by his older brother slip away. Through magic power he walks along the bottom of the sea. As he walks, he feeds the fishes. When he comes to a dirty little house in which there is a filthy old woman, he cleans the house, bathes the woman, builds a fire, and gives her food. She tells him where to find the fish he is looking for and gives him a stick of sugarcane, which she tells him to plant when he gets back home. However, his older brother eats the sugarcane and is sent to get another one. He does find the old woman, but he refuses to help her, and on his return journey, he loses his way and is drowned. "Two Brothers and Their Enmity," from *African Folk Tales with Foreign Analogues* by May Augusta Klipple (Department of English, Ball State Teacher's College, Muncie, Ind., Ph.D thesis, 1938).

Motifs:
Q2.1.2C - kind and unkind girls encounters en route subtype with pursuit
N789.1 - river carries off an object which the heroine pursues
Q41 - general politeness
W10 - kindness
Q40 - kindness rewarded
D1610 - magic talking objects
D1610.35 - speaking river
N825.3 - old woman encountered en route [girl heals her]
W27 - gratitude
D1658.3.4 - being encountered helps heroine [hides her]
D1520. - magic object which aids in return journey
J2415. - foolish imitation of lucky man
W198 - unkindness
Q280 - unkindness punished

TWO BROTHERS & THEIR ENMITY-West African variant
Q2 - kind and unkind
F420 - water spirit encountered
F133 - submarine otherworld
W10 - kindness
Q40 - kindness rewarded
Q41.2 - reward for cleansing loathsome person
W198 - unkindness
Q280 - unkindness punished
Q428 - punishment: drowning

15. The Gift of the Mermaid

CELTIC, BRITTANY

A long time ago, mermaids would rise from the waves on the Breton shores. They were often seen on moonlit nights combing their long hair, and occasionally they would come ashore in daylight and spread on the sand beautiful white linens covered with precious treasures — pearl necklaces, rings of all kinds, and jewels. It was believed that they found these treasures from sunken ships on the ocean floor. If anyone approached them, they would wrap up the treasure in their white linen cloths and quickly dive into the sea.

One day two young girls were walking on the beach gathering shells. They were surprised and excited to see a mermaid so busy playing with her treasure that she did not notice the two girls. They tiptoed toward her. When they were right in front of her, she looked up, but she did not grab her treasure and plunge into the sea. She smiled at the two little girls and said, "I would like to give you each a present." Then she quickly put something in each of two small white linen cloths and handed one to each girl. "This is my gift. Put it in your pocket and be sure not to open it until you are home with your parents."

The two girls thanked her. Then she said, "Now go to your family, and remember, do not open your gift until you are in your home." The girls ran off. When they turned to look back, the mermaid waved and dove into the sea.

One of the girls said, "Why wait until we are home? I want to see the treasure the mermaid gave me."

But the second girl said, "She told us to wait until we were home with our parents."

"I don't care," said the first girl, and she sat on a rock and opened her bundle. But inside there was only dirt. "Throw your bundle away," she said to her friend. "It was only a trick. There is only dirt inside."

But the other little girl took her bundle home. Her family watched as she opened it. It was filled with sparkling jewels!

> *Every soul is the hostage of its own deeds.*
>
> Koran 74:38

Story Notes:

The French word for "sea" is *mer*, thus, a mermaid is a maiden of the sea. The Breton word for sea is "mor" and one of the Breton words for mermaid is "morganez," which links them to the Morrigan, the triple goddess of death/wisdom in Ireland and to Modrona, the Queen Mother of Welsch tradition. The morganez are believed to have the power to heal, to hurt, help or hinder.

For more mermaid tales, see *A Treasury of Mermaids: Mermaid Tales from around the World,* collected and retold by Shirley Climo, with illustrations by Jean and Mou-Sien Tseng (HarperCollins, 1997).

ACTIVITY: Here is a magical effect to use when you retell this story!

Assemble four white linen dinner napkins. Be sure to wear a jacket with a pocket on each side. Put one napkin filled with dirt in your left pocket and one filled with "jewels" in your right pocket. For jewels, you can use the colored pieces of glass available in stained-glass stores or, more economically, the flattened glass marbles available in aquarium shops. Spread the empty napkins out as you tell the part of the story in which the mermaid is preparing the gifts. Pass your hand over the napkins as if you were putting something inside, quickly fold up each napkin, and put the napkins in your left pocket (which already has a napkin in it). Later, when you pull the napkin with jewels from one pocket and the one with dirt from your other pocket, no one will notice that you reached in different pockets; they will be intent on listening as you act natural and continue your story. This has a surprisingly magical effect. After telling the story, I like to hand out a jewel to everyone in the audience to take home as a memento.

Motifs:

Q2.1. - Kind and unkind. Kind and unkind girls.

F348.0.1 - fairy gift disappears or is turned to something worthless when tabu is broken

B81 - Mermaid

W26 - patience

Q64 - patience rewarded

Q111.7 - jewels as reward

Q580 - punishment fitted to crime [sand instead of jewels]

16. Anansi and His Son

ASHANTI, AFRICA

Kwaku Anansi, spider man, and his child Ntukuma lived on a farm, where they grew food. When harvesting time came, Anansi told Ntukuma to go away. "Why?" Ntukuma asked. "I did all this work with you. I worked on the farm with you, and now that the food is ready to harvest, why do you drive me away?" And Anansi said, "I don't care! I said go. I don't want to see you again!" So Ntukuma said, "All right. I'm going now."

He walked on down the road, wondering, "Where should I go? I'm hungry. I don't know what is going to happen to me." Then he heard somebody calling, "Ntukuma, come."

He couldn't tell where the voice was coming from. He called out, "Who is calling me? Where are you?"

The voice said, "You come down here."

So he went down that way. When he got down there, he saw a village, but he did not see any people. "Who is here?" he asked, and he heard from inside a house, "Come, I'm here."

When he went in the house, he saw a big woman, bigger than any woman he had ever seen before. And Ntukuma was afraid because she was too big. The woman said, "Don't be afraid of me. Tell me, why have you come to this place?" And Ntukuma replied, "My father sent me away because he did not want to have me eat our food."

She said, "Stay here. I will give you food."

He said, "All right."

That big woman said to him, "Go to my farm. You will see many things growing there. Some of the vegetables will talk and say, 'Take me, take me, take me.' Don't take those. When you hear some saying, 'Don't take me, don't take me, don't take me,' those are the ones you bring back."

Ntukuma went to the farm and heard vegetables calling out, "Take me." He did not pick them. Others said, "Don't take me." Those he took and brought back to the house. He made a big pot of soup. Then he asked the woman for some meat to put in the soup. She said, "Lift me up over the top of the soup pot. Then any kind of meat you like will be in the soup." He did this, and meat was in the soup. He ate with the woman. He slept there. He stayed there three days.

On the third day, he said, "Mammy, I need to go home. Will you give me some food for my journey?"

The woman answered, "My food can't go to your country, but I will give you a small drum. When you go to your country, your drum will give you any kind of food that you want." She gave him a small drum, and he left.

When he got home, Kwaku Anansi was not there. Ntukuma beat his drum three times, and Anansi heard. Ntukuma saw that suddenly there was a lot of food in the house. Before he had a chance to start eating, he saw his father coming from the bush. Anansi said, "Now I see my good child. You have brought us some different food." And he sat down and ate with Ntukuma. When they finished eating, he asked, "Where did you get this drum?" Ntukuma said, "I can't tell you." They slept. In the morning he made food again, the same way, by beating the drum. He ate with his father.

The boy decided he would go back to that big woman. He was afraid of his father. His father was always following him around.

Anansi was thinking, "Wherever this boy goes, I will follow him. I want that drum."

The next day, the boy started out early in the morning. He did not want his father to see him leave. He didn't know that Anansi was following him. Just as he reached the house country, he saw Anansi. Anansi called out, "Oh, I see a big woman. I never saw anything like her before. Where is this woman from?"

The woman said, "Ntukuma, did you bring this wicked man here?"

The woman said, "Anansi, go to my farm. You will hear vegetables call out to you, 'Take me, take me, take me.' Don't take those. You will see one vegetable that will say, 'Don't take me, don't take me, don't take me.' That is the one to bring back."

When Anansi went to the farm, he heard many vegetables saying, "Take me. Take me." And he said, "I am going to take those!" When he put them in the water for soup, they turned to stones. Then the woman sent Ntukuma to the farm. He brought back vegetables and made soup. Then the woman said to Ntukuma, "Carry me over the soup. Any kind of meat you want will be in this soup." Ntukuma did this, and he saw a lot of meat in the soup. They all ate together — Ntukuma, Anansi, and that woman. Then they slept.

The next day, Anansi said, "You are a very big woman. When you die, there will be a lot of meat because you are so big."

The woman said, "Ntukuma, take your father and go. He is very rude; I don't want to see him here."

Anansi said, "All right. I will go if you give me a drum. A drum that will bring food."

The woman said, "Go into the next room. There is a small drum there. Take that."

Anansi went to the next room and saw a lot of drums. He took the biggest one. Then he left to go home.

When he got home, however, he said, "Today I will feast!" and he beat his drum. When he beat that drum, hundreds of snakes appeared, and Anansi ran away. The snakes bit Anansi's wife. Fortunately, that woman had shown Ntukuma how to make medi- cine for snakebites, and he was able to cure his mother. After that, the people had medicine for snakebites; that is how people got medicine for snakebites.

That's all there is.

Speak in silver, answer in gold.

Swahili proverb

Story Notes:

Anansi the spider man is a trickster hero in West Africa. Like Coyote in many American Indian tales, Anansi is often greedy and foolish.

In many West African countries, children's names may be associated with events or the day of birth. Kwaku means "Thursday".

Folklorist Kate Kelly points out that the old woman is probably a snake. She lives underground, tells Ntukuma to "come down here," and at the end of the story has shown Ntukuma how to make medicine for snakebites. Kelly cites motif B512: Medicine shown by animal. One animal heals another with a medicine and teaches the remedy. The animal is most frequently the serpent. (See motif B491.1: helpful serpent.)

This story was originally published with the title "Pot and Whip." It is obviously related to another Anansi story in which Anansi touches a forbidden pot and a cord comes out and whips him. (See *Ananse the Spider: Tales from an Ashanti Village*, Peggy Appiah. N.Y.: Pantheon, 1966.) Kelly notes that a whipping cord is a metaphor for the snake, or vice-versa.

Here is another African story that involves choosing between foods, but in this story the choice is more clearly linked to motif L 210: choosing the humbler choice, as well as Q 3: modest request rewarded; immoderate punished.

A man has two sons, the older of whom continually insults his mother. The younger son is kind and courteous. The younger son visits his uncle, who welcomes him. The child eats politely, and when the uncle shows him a couch for resting, lies down and sleeps. When the boy is ready to return home, the uncle shows him some eggs and asks him to choose one. The boy takes a little egg and leaves the large eggs. The uncle tells him to break the egg near his home. When the boy does this, out of the egg come houses, animals, and people. The people make the boy their king. The older boy goes to see the uncle and is received as kindly as his brother, but he complains about the food and having to sleep on the couch. He chooses a large egg, and when he breaks it, soldiers come out and kill him. ("The Brothers and the Eggs," Mangbettu: Vekens, La Langue des Makers, des Medje et des Mangbetu, pp. 102ff., No. 4, "Un recit? Raconte." in May Augustine Klippie, *African Folk Tales with Foreign Analogues* (Muncie, Ind.: Ball State Teacher's College, Department of English, 1938), 366-368. Ph.D. thesis (microfilm). Tale # 54.

Pikkin, a West African term for "child," became pickaninny, in the vernacular of African Americans. When used by non African Americans the term is abrasive and prejudicial.

Here is the way this story was told by the storyteller to the collector. This is called "Pidgin English".

Kwaku Anansi an' his pikin [child] Ntukuma he go make big fa'rm. An' fa'rm he come in chop (food) plenty. When Anansi see dat chop

come in de fa'rm plenty, he tell Ntukuma go away, he tell him, say, "I don' wan' to see you." Ntukuma ask his father, "Why? I make trouble wit you, make dis fa'rm wit' you, and now you see chop, you drive me away?" An Anansi say, "I don' care! I say go, I don' wan' see you again!" An' Ntukuma say, "All right. I'm goin' now."

When he start go in de road, he go small faraway, an' he begin speak, "Which way I'm going to pass now? I'm hungry. I don' know what I'm goin' pass." Ntukuma say so. He hear somebody calling, "Ntukuma, Ntukuma, come."

He don' know de place de man calling from, an' Ntukuma ask him, "Whose place you stay an' call me?"

"You come down heah."

An' he go down de. When he go down de, he saw some village, an' he no see any pe'son de, an' Ntukuma ask who de in dis place, an' he answer him for de inside of he house. "Come, I'm here."

When he wen' in de house, he go saw big 'ooman, too big. No see so befo'. And when Ntukuma saw he begin to fea' because he too big. And de woman say, "Don' fea me." An' he ask him, "Why you cause me to come in de place?" An' he say, "My father sen' me away for de chop sake."

She say, "Stay here. I give you many of chop."

He say, "All right."

When he stay wit' hum, dat big 'ooman said to him, "Go my fa'rm. You go see some syam [food] there. You go see one go talk, 'Take me, take me, take me.' Don' take 'um. You go see one go speak, 'Don' take me, don' take me, don' take me.' Him you go bring."

He went fa'rm, and saw de nyam. Some said, "Teki me." He refuse. Some said, "Don' teki me." Den he go and tek' ' im, bring in house, put in fire, finally finish de fire, he put soup in de fire. He ask dat big ' ooman to give him meat in de soup. He say, "Carry me on top of de soup. Any kind meat you like will come inside de soup." He do same. He see any kind meat he like wit' de soup. Make chop, he chop with dat 'ooman. He sleep de. He stay about t'ree day. He used to chop wit' him.

T'ree days after, he say, "Mammy, I be goin'. ' Low, give me small chop, I go my country."

The woman answer him dat "My chop can' go to your country, but I give you small drum. Dis drum when I give you, when you go to your country, any kind chop you want, your drum will give you." He give him small drum so, take go he country.

When he get de, Kwaktu Anansi no de. He fo fa'rm he fadder. He beati de drum t'ree times. Anansi hea' de law somebody beati de drum for his country. He, Ntukuma, see plenty chop. Before he go chop, he see he fadder come for bush. He say, "Now I see mu good pikin. You bring some different chop." An' he come an' chop wit' Ntukuma. When he chop finish, he say, "Which place you get dis drum?" Ntukuma say, "I can' tell you." He sleep. Mornin' time he make same chop, da same drum. He chop wit' he fadder.

Dat boy t'ink for he head her wan' go back to dat big 'ooman, he fea' he fadder too much. Sometime he go an' he follow him and spoil it.

Den Anansi too t'ink in he head, "When dis boy go I will folli him."

Nex' day, boy sta't quick, sta't mornin' sharp. He no wan' he fadder see him. He don' know dat'Anansi follow him. Before he reach de house country, he go looki about he, see Anansi. Anansi begin say, "Oh, I see big 'ooman, I no see before. What dis' 'ooman from?"

De 'ooman say, "Ntukuma, you bring dis' wicket man hea?"

De 'ooman tell Anansi, say, "Go bring some chop in my fa'rm. You go see one nyam de call you, 'Take me, take me, take me.' No teki 'em. You go see one nyam de call you, 'Don' take me, don' take me, don' take me.' Take him come."

When Anansi wen' to fa'rm, he saw nyam say "Take me," "I go teki dat nyam!" He go tek' da' one. When he put him for de fire, coming stone. When he coming stone, he (woman) sent Ntukuma say, "Go take nyam." He go bring 'em, good nyam, put fire. De 'ooman tell him, "Carry me for dis coup, any kind meat you wan', you go see for dis soup." Do same. He see lot of meat in soup, chop togedder wit' Anansi an' dat 'ooman. Sleep de.

Nes' day, Anansi say, "You dis' big 'ooman, when you die, you go see many of meat, because you're too big."

An' dat 'ooman tell Ntukuma, "Tak' yo' fadder go. I don' wan' see him hea'."

Anansi say, "All right, give me some drum. When I go I get chop."

That 'ooman say, "Go inside disi room. Small drum de, teki him." Anansi went de. See lot of drum de. He go take big one, take for his country. When he go he country, he say, "Today I go chop too much." An' he beat dat drum. When he beat dat drum, he see plenty snake come in Anansi town, wan' catch him. Anansi run away for bush. Before he de come for de 'ooman country, 'ooman show Ntukuma some medicine for snake, when snake take somebody. In town of Anansi snake go catch Anansi wife. Ntukuma go meki medicine for him. Dis cause people got medicine of snake.

Da's all dis.

Motifs:

S222 - child abandoned[driven forth, exposed]

F92 - pit entrance to lower world

F92.7 - hole to underworld kingdom of snakes

F127.1 - journey to serpent kingdom

H935 - encounters old woman or witch ["biggest woman ever seen"]

D1610 - magic talking objects

C811.2 - yams[vegetables] say take me/don't take me

W31 - obedience

D1472.2 - magic food-supplier

D1658.3.2 - advised which reward to choose

W15. - greed

Q2.1.4 - punishment: snakes [Anansi's magic drum holds snakes]

B511.1 - snake as healer

17. The Three Girls and the Journey-Cakes

APPALACHIA, UNITED STATES

A widow woman who could make good journey-cakes had three girls. Be they pretty or ugly, I don't recollect. Anyhow, they lived at home till they got to be women grown and thought they could make their own way in the wide world.

The oldest girl said one day, "I aim to go out in the wide world to seek my fortune. Could you fix me a snack to eat on the journey to wherever I aim to go?"

Her mammy baked two journey-cakes. "You can have your druthers," she said to the oldest girl. "Will you take the biggest journey-cake with my curse or the least journey-cake with my blessing?"

"I aim to take the biggest journey-cake," was what the oldest girl said she wanted. And she wrapped it up in her Sunday best plaid shawl — blue and red and yellow it was — and set out on her long journey. Whenever it was time to eat, the birds and the other wood creatures gathered round where she sat down under some trees to eat. They asked polite as you please would she give them a crumb, maybe two. "No," she said, "I won't give you none. I hardly got aplenty for my own self." So she kept all her big journey-cake for herself.

She traveled on till she came to a house where she hired herself out to watch by the side of a dead man, so that his sister who had stayed with him till he died could get some sleep. Her wages were named to her — a peck of gold and a peck of silver and a bottle of liniment that would even cure a dead person.

All through the daytime she slept in a soft bed with a silk coverlet spread over her. When night came on, she sat down by the dead man to watch. She went to sleep on the job, and the dead man's sister hit her over the head with a stick and killed her, throwing her out in the high weeds and grass in the meadow.

Time passed by and the oldest girl didn't come home to the widow woman's house. So the middle girl said, "I aim to go out in the wide world to seek my fortune. Could you fix me a snack to eat on the journey to wherever I aim to go?"

Her mammy baked two journey-cakes. "You can have your druthers," she said to the middle girl. "Will you take the biggest journey-cake with my curses or the least journey-cake with my blessings?"

"I aim to take the biggest journey-cake," was what the middle girl said she wanted. And she wrapped it up in her Sunday best plaid shawl — all green and blue it was — and set out on her long journey. Whenever it was time to eat, the birds and the other wood creatures gathered round where she sat down under some trees to eat. They asked polite as you please would she give them a crumb, maybe two. "No," she said, "I won't give you none. I hardly got aplenty for my own self." So she kept all her big journey-cake for herself.

She traveled on till she came to a house where she hired herself out to watch by the side of a dead man, so that his sister, who had stayed with him till he died, could get some sleep. Her wages were named to her, a peck of gold and a peck of silver and a bottle of liniment that would even cure a dead person.

All through the daytime she slept in a soft bed with a silk coverlet spread over her. When night came on, she sat down by the dead man to watch. She went to sleep on the job, and the dead man's sister hit her over the head with a stick and killed her, throwing her out in the high weeds and grass in the meadow.

Time passed by and the middle girl didn't come home to the widow woman's house. The widow woman got worried and cried, having lost two of her girls out in the wide world. The youngest girl was gentle-natured, and she said, "Please, Mammy, hush up your crying, and I'll go look for your two girls that's lost. And I'd be much obliged if you would fix me a little snack to eat along the way on my journey out in the wide world."

Her mammy baked two journey-cakes — a big one and a little bitty one with the scrapings of the dough. "You can have your druthers," she said to the least girl. "Will you take the biggest journey-cake with my curses or the little bitty journey-cake with my blessings?"

"I wouldn't set out on a journey without your blessing," the least girl said. "And the little bitty journey-cake will be plenty big for me." She wrapped the little bitty journey-cake in her old grey shawl and set out on her journey.

When it was time to eat, she called the birds and the woods creatures about her before she unwrapped her journey-cake and sat down to eat. "Won't you have some?" she said and passed it around till she had no more than a crumb or two left for her own self. Then she got up and walked on, and the birds and other woods creatures went along with her, though they kept hidden in the edge of the woods and didn't show themselves.

It turned out that she hired herself to do the same job her sisters had tried their luck with. Her wages were named to her, a peck of gold and a peck of silver and a bottle of liniment that would even cure a dead person.

All though the day she slept in a soft bed with a silk coverlet spread over her. When night came on, she sat down by the dead man to watch. The little birds — the night birds — sat outside the window and kept her awake. After a time, the dead man rose up in the bed. "If you don't lay down and stay dead, I aim to hit you with this strap," she said. And he lay back down.

Time passed and the dead man rose up again. The youngest girl hit him with a strap and made him lie down dead. Three times he rose up, and the last time he jumped out of bed, and she took out after him. Woods creatures carried her on their backs. The little birds whirled about the dead man's head, and the little woods creatures got under his feet and tripped him up, so after a time he gave up and lay down and stayed dead. Then the youngest girl went back to his sister's house and collected her wages, a peck of gold and a peck of silver and a bottle of liniment that would even cure a dead person.

She hunted around in the high weeds and grass in the meadow till she found her sisters lying there dead. She rubbed the liniment on them till they came to life. Then they all three went home again, and the widow woman made them welcome and they lived off the youngest girl's wages, all their lives, I reckon. A peck of gold and a peck of silver would last mighty long time if a person never spent lavish.

Actions speak louder than words.

U.S. proverb

Story Notes:

Music and storytelling are part of the Appalachian culture, undoubtedly a reflection of the many Irish and Scottish immigrant settlers. This story is told in the storyteller's dialect. As the stories were handed down by word of mouth, they often were changed by the teller.

The colors in the shawls reveal the status of each girl. Note that the oldest girl's shawl is plaid, a vestige of this version's Irish origin. The payment, "a peck of silver and a peck of gold," are the same in this story and in the Scottish variant, "The Girl and the Dead Man." page 146. In addition, the journey with the dead man is almost identical.

In many fairy tales, when the unkind sister (or sisters) does not share food, she is often turned into a stone or other inanimate object. If you are not in touch with your feelings, the story seems to say, you are stone-hearted. The boy or girl that shares food and drink, receives good advice in exchange. A characteristic of the folk tale genre is that actions and objects reveal the inner workings of the characters. Being turned to stone or other inanimate object is a literal depiction, symbolically showing that they are cut off from feelings and emotions. In this story, by sharing her food, the girl created a situation that helped her.

Motifs:

J229.3 - large cake with curse, or small with blessing
L222 - modest choice: parting gift
H1550 - test of character
D754.1 - disenchantment by guarding sleeping man
Q2.1 - kind and unkind girls
L210 - modest choice
H1199.1 - heroine must sit up with a corpse
H1550 - test of character
D754.1 - disenchantment by guarding sleeping man
Q81 - reward for perseverance
Q140 - marvelous or magic reward
B300 - helpful animals - general
B430 - helpful wild beasts
B450 - helpful birds
Q150 - immunity from disaster as reward [liniment = water of life?]
Q280 - unkindness punished

18. The Corpse Watchers

WEXFORD, IRELAND

here was once a poor woman who had three daughters, and one day the eldest said, "Mother, bake my cake and kill my cock, till I go seek my fortune." So her mother did, and when all was ready, says her mother to her, "Which will you have, half of these with my blessing, or the whole with my curse?"

"Curse or no curse," says she, "the whole is little enough." So away she set, and if the mother didn't give her curse, she didn't give her blessing. The girl walked and she walked till she was tired and hungry, and then she sat down to take her dinner. While she was eating it, a poor woman came up and asked for a bit. "The dickens a bit you'll get from me," says she. "It's all too little for myself." And the poor woman walked away very sorrowful .

At nightfall the girl got lodging at a farmer's, and the woman of the house told her that she'd give her a spadeful of gold and a shovelful of silver if she'd only sit up and watch her son's corpse that was waking in the next room. She said she'd do that. And so, when the family were in their bed, she sat by the fire and cast an eye from time to time on the corpse that was lying under the table.

All at once the dead man got up in his shroud and stood before her and said, "All alone, fair maid!" She gave him no answer, and when he said it the third time, he struck her with a switch, and she became a grey flag.

About a week after, the second daughter went to seek her fortune, and she didn't care for her mother's blessing any more than her sister had, and the very same thing happened to her. She was left a grey flag by the side of the other.

At last the youngest went off in search of the other two, and she took care to carry her mother's blessing with her. She shared her dinner with the poor woman on the road, and the woman told her that she would watch over her.

Well, she got lodging in the same place as the others, and agreed to mind the corpse. She sat up by the fire with the dog and cat and amused herself with some apples and nuts the mistress gave her. She thought it a pity that the man under the table was a corpse, he was so handsome.

But at last he got up, and says he, "All alone, fair maid!" And she wasn't long about an answer.

"All alone I am not. I've a little dog and Pussy, the cat. I've apples to roast and nuts to crack, All alone I am not."

"Ho, ho!" says he, "you're a girl of courage, though you wouldn't have enough to follow me. I am now going to cross the quaking bog and go through the burning forest. I must then enter the cave of terror, and climb the hill of glass, and drop from the top of it into the Dead Sea."

"I will follow you," says she, "for I engaged to mind you." He thought to prevent her, but she was as determined. Out he sprang through the window, and she followed him till they came to the Green Hills, and then says he: "Open, open, Green Hills, and let the Light of the Green Hills through."

"Aye," says the girl, "and let the fair maid, too."

They opened, and the man and girl passed through, and there they were, on the edge of a bog.

He trod lightly over the shaky bits of moss and sod. And while she was thinking of how she'd get across, the old beggar woman appeared to her, but much nicer dressed, and touched her shoes with her stick, and the soles spread a foot on each side. So she easily got over the shaky marsh.

The burning wood was at the edge of the bog, and there the old woman flung a damp, thick cloak over her, and through the flames she went, and not a hair of her head was singed.

Then they passed through the dark cavern of horrors, where she'd have heard the most horrible yells, only that the old woman, who was really a fairy, stopped her ears with wax. She saw frightful things, with blue vapors round them, and felt the sharp rocks and the slimy backs of frogs and snakes.

When they got out of the cavern, they were at the mountain of glass. And then the fairy made her slippers so sticky with a tap of her rod that she followed the young corpse easily to the top. There was the deep sea a quarter of a mile under them, and so the corpse said to her, "Go home to my mother, and tell her how far you've come to do my bidding. Farewell." He sprung head foremost down into the sea, but after him she plunged, without stopping a moment to think about it.

She was stupefied at first, but when they reached the waters, she recovered her thoughts. After piercing down a great depth, they saw a green light toward the bottom. At last they were below the sea; it seemed a green sky above them. They were sitting in a beautiful meadow, she half asleep and her head resting against his side. She couldn't keep her eyes open and couldn't tell how long she had slept, but when she woke, she was in bed at his house, and he and his mother were sitting at her bedside and watching her.

Then she learned that a witch who had a spite to the young man because he wouldn't marry her had kept him in a state between life and death till a young woman would rescue him by doing what she had done.

So at her request her sisters got their own shapes again and were sent back to their mother with their spades of gold and shovels of silver. Maybe they were better after that, but I doubt it much.

The younger one got the young gentleman as her husband. I'm sure she deserved him, and if they didn't live happily, that we may!

Story Notes:

The girl in this variant displays active heroism coupled with compassion. An unusual component of this text is that the punishment for the girls who fail to behave properly is temporary and reversed; all the girls return home with gifts. This is also true in the Appalachian variant, "The Three Girls and the Journey-Cakes" page 70, obviously derived from this Scottish source. Both of these tales demonstrate the power of the mother's blessing. The mother's blessing also plays an important role in a Russian tale, "Baba Yaga," protecting a little girl sent by her stepmother to visit the witch known as Baba Yaga. In a similar variant, "The Girl and the Dead Man" page 146, a magical stick has a different function, causing the girl to adhere to the corpse on his journey.

Celtic scholar Laura Fadave notes that staying with a body overnight, the Wake, is part of Irish tradition. Commonly, games were played to honor the dead - to affirm the link between the living and dead. In Celtic myth, water is the primary elemental link between This World and the Otherworld. Bogs, as with any watery landscape were associated with ritual activity. And since ambiguity and multiplicity of meaning are features of Celtic lore, bogs which often appear to be firm ground, have a special power.

The hill of glass resonates with the Mountain of Glass in "The Birth of Lugh" from the Irish *Mythological Cycle*.

Motifs:

L222 - modest choice: parting gift

H1550 - test of character

J229.3 - large cake with curse, or small with blessing

D754.1 - disenchantment by guarding sleeping man.

Q2.1 - kind and unkind girls

L54 - compassionate youngest daughter

H1199.1 - heroine must sit up with a corpse

Q42.1.1 - child divides last loaf with fairy(witch, etc.)

Q1.1 - gods (saints) in disguise reward hospitality, punish inhospitality

F234.2 - fairy in form of person

B822 - magic wand or stick

F212 - fairyland under water

Q81 - perseverance

D700 - person disenchanted

L162 - favorable marriage as reward

19. The Old Hag's Long Leather Bag

IRELAND

Once on a time, long, long ago, there was a widow woman who had three daughters. When their father died, their mother thought they would never want, for he had left her a long leather bag filled with gold and silver. But he was not long dead when an old hag came begging to the house one day and stole the leather bag filled with gold and silver and went away out of the country with it, no one knew where.

So from that day, the widow woman and her three daughters were poor, and she had a hard struggle to live and to bring up her three daughters.

But when they were grown up, the eldest said one day, "Mother, I'm a young woman now, and it's a shame for me to be here doing nothing to help you or myself. Bake me a bannock and cut me a dollop, till I go away to push my luck."

The mother baked her a whole bannock and asked her if she would take half of it with her blessing on it or the whole without. She said to give her the whole bannock without.

So she took it and went away. She told them if she was not back in a year and a day from that, then they would know she was doing well and making her fortune.

She traveled away and away before her, far further than I can tell you, and twice as far as you could tell me, until she came to a strange country, and going up to a little house, she found an old hag living in it. The hag asked her where she was going. She said she was going to push her fortune.

Said the hag, "How would you like to stay with me, for I want a maid?"

"What will I have to do?"

"You will have to wash me and dress me and sweep the hearth clean; but on the peril of your life, never look up the chimney," said the hag.

"All right," she agreed to this.

The next day, when the hag arose, the girl washed her and dressed her, and when the hag went out, she swept the hearth clean, and she thought it would be no harm to have one wee look up the chimney. And there what did she see but her own mother's long leather bag of gold and silver? So she took it down at once, and getting it on her back, started away for home as fast as she could run.

But she had not gone far when she met a horse grazing in a field, and when he saw her, he said, "Rub me! Rub me! For I haven't been rubbed these seven years."

But she only struck him with a stick she had in her hand and drove him out of her way.

She had not gone much further when she met a sheep, who said, "Oh, shear me! Shear me! For I haven't been shorn these seven years."

But she struck the sheep and sent it scurrying out of her way.

She had not gone much further when she met a tethered goat, who said, "Oh, change my tether. Change my tether. For it hasn't been changed these seven years."

But she flung a stone at him and went on.

Next she came to a limekiln, and it said, "Oh, clean me! Clean me! For I haven't been cleaned these seven years."

But she only scowled at it and hurried on.

After awhile she met a cow, and it said, "Oh, milk me! Milk me! For I haven't been milked these seven years."

She struck the cow out of her way and went on.

Then she came to a mill. The mill said, "Oh, turn me. Turn me! For I haven't been turned these seven years."

But she did not pay heed what it said, only went in and lay behind the mill door with the bag under her head, for it was then night.

When the hag came into her hut again and found the girl gone, she ran to the chimney and looked up to see if she had carried off the bag. She got into a great rage, and she started to run as fast as she could after her.

She had not gone far when she met the horse, and she said, "Oh, horse, horse of mine, did you see this little maid of mine, with my tig, with my tag, with my long leather bag and all the gold and silver I have earned since I was a maid?"

"Aye," said the horse, "it is not long since she passed here."

So on she ran, and it was not long till she met the sheep and said she, "Sheep, sheep of mine, did you see this little maid of mine, with my tig, with my tag, with my long leather bag and all the gold and silver I have earned since I was a maid?"

"Aye," said the sheep, "it is not long since she passed here."

So the hag went on, and it was not long before she met the goat, and said she, "Goat, goat of mine. Did you see this little maid of mine, with my tig, with my tag, with my long leather bag and all the gold and silver I have earned since I was a maid?"

"Aye, it is not long since she passed here."

So she went on, and it was not long before she met the limekiln, and said she, "Did you see this little maid of mine, with my tig, with my tag, with my long leather bag and all the gold and silver I have earned since I was a maid?"

"Aye, it is not long since she passed here."

So she went on and it was not long before she met the cow, and said she, "Did you see this little maid of mine, with my tig, with my tag, with my long leather bag and all the gold and silver I have earned since I was a maid?"

"Aye, it is not long since she passed here."

So she went on, and it was not long before she met the mill, and said she, "Did you see this little maid of mine, with my tig, with my tag, with my long leather bag and all the gold and silver I have earned since I was a maid?"

And the mill said, "Yes, she is sleeping behind the door."

So the hag went in and struck the girl with a white rod and turned her into stone. She then took the bag of gold and silver on her back and went away back home.

A year and a day had gone by after the eldest daughter left home, and when she had not returned, the second daughter got up, and she said, "My sister must be doing well and making her fortune, and isn't it a shame for me to be sitting here doing nothing, wither to help you, mother, or myself? Bake me a bannock," said she, "and cut me a dollop, till I go away to push my luck."

The mother did this and asked the girl if she would have half of it with her blessing on it or the whole without. The girl said to give her the whole bannock without.

So she took it and went away. She told them if she was not back in a year and a day from that, then they would know she was doing well and making her fortune.

She traveled away and away before her, far further than I can tell you, and twice as far as you could tell me, until she came to a strange country, and going up to a little house, she found an old hag living in it. The hag asked her where she was going. She said she was going to push her fortune.

Said the hag, "How would you like to stay with me, for I want a maid?"

"What will I have to do?"

"You will have to wash me and dress me and sweep the hearth clean; but on the peril of your life, never look up the chimney," said the hag.

"All right," she agreed to this.

The next day, when the hag arose, the girl washed her and dressed her, and when the hag went out, she swept the hearth clean, and she thought it would be no harm to have one wee look up the chimney. And there what did she see but her own mother's long leather bag of gold and silver? So she took it down at once and, getting it on her back, started away for home as fast as she could run.

But she had not gone far when she met a horse grazing in a field, and when he saw her, he said, "Rub me! Rub me! For I haven't been rubbed these seven years."

But she only struck him with a stick she had in her hand and drove him out of her way.

She had not gone much further when she met a sheep, who said, "Oh, shear me! Shear me! For I haven't been shorn these seven years."

But she struck the sheep and sent it scurrying out of her way.

She had not gone much further when she met a tethered goat, who said, "Oh, change my tether. Change my tether. For it hasn't been changed these seven years."

But she flung a stone at him and went on.

Next she came to a limekiln, and it said, "Oh, clean me! Clean me! For I haven't been cleaned these seven years."

But she only scowled at it and hurried on.

After a while she met a cow, and it said, "Oh, milk me! Milk me! For I haven't been milked these seven years."

She struck the cow out of her way and went on.

Then she came to a mill. The mill said, "Oh, turn me. Turn me! For I haven't been turned these seven years."

But she did not pay heed what it said, only went in and lay behind the mill door with the bag under her head, for it was then night.

When the hag came into her hut again and found the girl gone, she ran to the chimney and looked up to see if she had carried off the bag. She got into a great rage, and she started to run as fast as she could after her.

She had not gone far when she met the horse, and she said, "Oh, horse, horse of mine, did you see this little maid of mine, with my tig, with my tag, with my long leather bag and all the gold and silver I have earned since I was a maid?"

"Aye," said the horse, "it is not long since she passed here."

So on she ran, and it was not long till she met the sheep and said she, "Sheep, sheep of mine, did you see this little maid of mine, with my tig, with my tag, with my long leather bag and all the gold and silver I have earned since I was a maid?"

"Aye," said the sheep, "it is not long since she passed here."

So she went on, and it was not long before she met the goat, and said she, "Goat, goat of mine, did you see this little maid of mine, with my tig, with my tag, with my long leather bag and all the gold and silver I have earned since I was a maid?"

"Aye, it is not long since she passed here."

So she went on and it was not long before she met the limekiln, and said she, "Did you see this little maid of mine, with my tig, with my tag, with my long leather bag and all the gold and silver I have earned since I was a maid?"

"Aye, it is not long since she passed here."

So she went on and it was not long before she met the cow, and said she, "Did you see this little maid of mine, with my tig, with my tag, with my long leather bag and all the gold and silver I have earned since I was a maid?"

"Aye, it is not long since she passed here."

So she went on, and it was not long before she met the mill, and said she, did you see this little maid of mine, with my tig, with my tag, with my long leather bag and all the gold and silver I have earned since I was a maid?"

And the mill said, "Yes, she is sleeping behind the door." So the hag went in and struck this girl as well with her white rod, which turned her into stone. Then she took the bag of gold and silver and went back home.

When the second daughter had been gone a year and a day and hadn't come back, the youngest daughter said, "My two sisters must be doing well and making their fortunes, and isn't it a shame for me to be sitting here doing nothing to help you, mother, or myself? Bake me a bannock," said she, "and cut me a dollop, till I go away to push my luck."

The mother baked her a whole bannock and asked her if she would have half of it with her blessing on it or the whole without. She said, "I will take half the bannock with your blessing, Mother."

The youngest girl traveled away and away before her, far further than I can tell you, and twice as far as you could tell me, until she came to a strange country, and going up to a little house, she found an old hag living in it. The hag asked her where she was going. She said she was going to push her fortune.

Said the hag, "How would you like to stay with me, for I want a maid?"

"What will I have to do?"

"You will have to wash me and dress me and sweep the hearth clean; but on the peril of your life, never look up the chimney," said the hag.

"All right," the girl agreed to this.

The next day, when the hag arose, the girl washed her and dressed her, and when the hag went out, she swept the hearth clean, and she thought it would be no harm to have one wee look up the chimney. And there what did she see but her own mother's long leather bag of gold and silver? So she took it down at once and, getting it on her back, started away for home as fast as she could run.

But she had not gone far when she met a horse grazing in a field, and when he saw her, he said, "Rub me! Rub me! For I haven't been rubbed these seven years."

"Oh, poor horse, poor horse," she said, "I'll surely do that." And she laid down her bag and rubbed the horse.

She had not gone much further when she met a sheep, who said, "Oh, shear me! Shear me! For I haven't been shorn these seven years."

"Oh, poor sheep," she said, "I'll surely do that." And she laid down her bag and cut the heavy wool from the sheep.

She had not gone much further when she met a tethered goat, and he said, "Oh, change my tether. Change my tether. For it hasn't been changed these seven years."

"Oh, poor goat," she said, "I'll surely do that." And she laid down her bag and changed the goat's leash.

Next she came to a limekiln, and it said, "Oh, clean me! Clean me! For I haven't been cleaned these seven years."

"Oh, poor limekiln," she said, "I'll surely do that." And she laid down her bag, and cleaned the kiln.

After a while she met a cow, and it said, "Oh, milk me! Milk me! For I haven't been milked these seven years."

"Oh, poor cow," she said, "I'll surely do that." And she laid down her bag and milked the cow.

Then she came to a mill. The mill said, "Oh, turn me. Turn me! For I haven't been turned these seven years."

"Oh, poor mill," she said, "I'll surely do that." And she laid down her bag and tended to the mill.

When the hag came into her hut again and found the girl gone, she ran to the chimney and looked up to see if she had carried off the bag. She got into a great rage, and she started to run as fast as she could after her.

She had not gone far when she met the horse, and she said, "Oh, horse, horse of mine, did you see this little maid of mine, with my tig, with my tag, with my long leather bag and all the gold and silver I have earned since I was a maid?"

The horse said, "Do you think I have nothing to do, only watch your maids for you? You may go somewhere else and look for her."

So on the hag ran, and it was not long till she met the sheep, and said she, "Sheep, sheep of mine, did you see this little maid of mine, with my tig, with my tag, with my long leather bag and all the gold and silver I have earned since I was a maid?"

The sheep said, "Do you think I have nothing to do, only watch your maids for you? You may go somewhere else and look for her."

So on she ran, and it was not long till she met the goat, and she said, "Goat, goat of mine, did you see this little maid of mine, with my tig, with my tag, with my long leather bag and all the gold and silver I have earned since I was a maid?"

The goat said, "Do you think I have nothing to do, only watch your maids for you? You may go somewhere else and look for her."

So on she ran, and it was not long till she met the limekiln and she said, "Limekiln, limekiln of mine, did you see this little maid of mine, with my tig, with my tag, with my long leather bag and all the gold and silver I have earned since I was a maid?"

The limekiln said, "Do you think I have nothing to do, only watch your maids for you? You may go somewhere else and look for her."

So on she ran, and it was not long till she met the cow, and said she, "Cow, cow of mine, did you see this little maid of mine, with my tig, with my tag, with my long leather bag and all the gold and silver I have earned since I was a maid?"

The cow said, "Do you think I have nothing to do, only watch your maids for you? You may go somewhere else and look for her."

So on she ran, and it was not long till she came to the mill, and she said, "Mill, mill of mine, did you see this little maid of mine, with my tig, with my tag, with my long leather bag and all the gold and silver I have earned since I was a maid?"

The mill said, "Come nearer and whisper to me."

She went nearer to whisper to the mill, and the mill dragged her under the wheels and ground her up.

The old hag had dropped the white rod out of hand, and the mill told the young girl to take this rod and strike two stones behind the mill door. When she did that, her two sisters stood up! She hoisted the leather bag on her back, and the three of them set out and traveled away and away till they reached home.

The mother had been crying all the time they were away and was now ever so glad to see them, and rich and happy they all lived after.

 Kindness is more binding than a loan.

Chinese proverb

Story Notes:

A bag is often depicted in sculptures with various Irish goddesses, notes Celtic scholar Laura Fadave. She suggests the gold and silver link this bag to the treasures of fairy gold.

Bannock cakes were used a means of divination. Like pulling the short straw, the one who chose the burnt piece of bannock was chosen for the task at hand.

Popular Appalachian variants of this story, appear as "Gallymanders," in *Grandfather Tales*, selected and edited by Richard Chase (Boston, Mass: Houghton Mifflin Company, 1948) pp.18-28; "The Gold in the Chimley" in *Buying the Wind*, ed. by Richard Dorson (Ill: University of Chicago Press, 1964) pp.206-209 (This story was originally collected by the renowned folklore collector Leonard Roberts and published in *Midwest Folklore*, volume six, number two (summer 1956), pp.76-78.) This story also appears as "Old Gally Manders" in *American Folk and Fairy Tales*, selected by Rachel Field (New York: Scribner's, 1929) and in *Witches, Witches, Witches*, by Helen Hoke (New York: Franklin Watts, 1958), pp. 15-18.

Motifs:

- Q2.1 - kind and unkind girls
- Q2.1.2 - encounters en route subtype.
- Q2.1.2C - pursuit Form
- Q2.1.2Cb - Long Leather Bag Group
- Q2.1.2Cbd - Long Leather Bag.
- L222 - modest choice: parting gift
- H1550 - test of character
- J229.3 - large cake with curse, or small with blessing
- C328 - heroine forbidden to look up chimney
- Q280 - unkindness punished
- B822 - magic wand or stick
- Q41 - kindness
- B350 - grateful animals
- B397 - donkey or horse grateful for being rubbed or washed
- B395 - sheep grateful for being sheared
- B394.2 - goat grateful for being milked or unleashed
- D1658.2.13 - a mill is turned
- D1658.3.4 - grateful objects help fugitive
- Q140 - marvelous or magic reward

20. The Three Heads of the Well

ENGLAND

ong before Arthur and the Knights of the Round Table, there reigned in the eastern part of England a king who kept his court at Colchester.

In the midst of all his glory, his queen died, leaving behind an only daughter, about fifteen years of age, who for her beauty and kindness was the wonder of all that knew her. But the king, hearing of a lady who had likewise an only daughter, had a mind to marry the lady for the sake of her riches, though she was old, ugly, hook nosed, and known to have an ill nature. The lady's daughter resembled her mother greatly. Nonetheless, in a few weeks after the first queen died, the king, attended by the nobility and gentry, had the marriage rites performed.

The new queen had not been long in the court before she set the king against his own beautiful daughter by telling him untrue things about her. The young princess, having lost her father's love, begged her father, with tears in her eyes, to let her go and seek her fortune, to which the king consented, and he ordered her stepmother to give her something for her journey. The queen gave her a canvas bag containing brown bread, hard cheese, and a bottle of ale. Though this was but a pitiful dowry for a king's daughter, she took it with thanks and proceeded on her journey, passing through groves, woods, and valleys till she came upon an old man sitting on a stone at the mouth of a cave.

He said, "Good morrow, fair maiden, whither away so fast?"

"Aged father," said she, "I am going to seek my fortune."

"What have you got in your bag and bottle?"

"In my bag I have bread and cheese, and in my bottle some ale. Would you like to have some?"

"Yes," said he, "with all my heart."

With that the girl pulled out her provisions and bade him eat. He did so, and gave her many thanks and said, "There is a thick thorny hedge before you, which you cannot get through, but take this wand in your hand, strike it three times, and say, 'Please, hedge, let me come through,' and it will open immediately. Then, a little further, you will find a well. Sit down on the wall around the well and there will come up three golden heads, which will speak. Do whatever they ask of you." Promising she would, she took her leave of him.

After a while she came to the hedge, and with her use of the old man's wand, it divided and let her through. Then, coming to the well, she had no sooner sat down than a golden head came up, singing:

"Wash me, and comb me,

And lay me down softly.

And lay me on a bank to dry,

That I may look pretty,

When somebody passes by."

"Yes, I will," said she, and taking the head in her lap, she combed it with a silver comb and then placed it upon a primrose bank.

Then up came a second and a third head, both saying the same as the first. So she did the same for them, and then she sat down to rest.

Then said the heads, one to another, "What shall we wish for this damsel who has used us so kindly?"

The first said, "I wish her to be so beautiful."

The second said, "I wish her such a sweet voice as shall far exceed the nightingale."

The third said, "As she is a king's daughter, I'll wish that she become a queen."

The girl helped them down into the well again and went on her journey. She had not traveled long before she saw a king hunting in the park with his nobles. She would have avoided him, but the king, catching sight of her, came to talk with her, and they fell desperately in love and decided to marry.

When the king learned that she was the king of Colchester's daughter, he ordered some chariots made ready so that they could visit her father. When the king, her father, saw her riding in a chariot adorned with rich gems of gold, he was astonished. And great was the joy at court amongst all, with the exception of the queen and her daughter, who were ready to burst with envy. Feasting and dancing continued many days. Then the girl left with her husband and the dowry her father had given her.

The other princess, seeing that her sister had been so lucky in seeking her fortune, wanted to do the same, so she told her mother, and all preparations were made. She was furnished with rich dresses, sugar, almonds, sweetmeats, and a large bottle of wine. With these she went down the same road as her sister. She saw the old man, who said, "Young woman, whither so fast?"

"What's that to you?" said she.

"Then," said he, "what have you in your bag and bottle?"

She answered, "Good things, which you shall not be troubled with."

"Won't you give me some?" he said.

"No, not a bit, nor a drop."

The old man frowned, saying, "Evil fortune attend ye!"

Walking on, she came to the hedge. She saw a gap and tried to pass through it, but the hedge closed, and the thorns cut into her flesh so that it was with great difficulty that she was able to finally get through the hedge. Then she searched for water to wash the blood off herself and, looking round, saw the well. When she sat down on the edge of the well, one of the heads came up, saying, "Wash me, comb me, and lay me down softly," but she handed it her wine bottle, saying,

"Use that for your washing." The second and third heads came up and met with the same treatment. Then the heads consulted among themselves what to do to this girl for her bad manners.

The first said, "Let her face be covered with sores."

The second said, "Let her voice be as harsh as a corncrake's."

The third said, "Let her be poor all of life."

The girl went on till she came to a town, where it happened to be market day. People avoided her when they saw her face and especially when they heard her squeaky voice. It happened, however, that a poor country cobbler was mending shoes for an old hermit, who said, "I have no money to give you, only this medicine for sores and this bottle of spirits to improve the voice."

The cobbler took these and, having a mind to do an act of charity, went up to the girl and asked her who she was. "I am," said she, "the king of Colchester's daughter."

"Well," said the cobbler, "if I restore you to your natural complexion and voice, will you in reward take me for a husband?"

"Yes, friend," replied she, "with all my heart!"

With this, the cobbler applied the remedies, and they made her well in a few weeks, after which they were married and set forth together for the court at Colchester.

When the queen found that her daughter had married nothing but a poor cobbler, she hung herself in wrath. The death of the queen pleased the king, who was glad to get rid of her. He gave the cobbler and his wife money and a place to live in a remote part of the kingdom, where they lived the rest of the days of their lives.

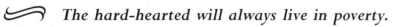 *The hard-hearted will always live in poverty.*

Hausa proverb

Story Notes:

This injustice at the beginning of the story is a typical motif in Tale Type 480. See "The Three Little Men in the Woods," page 29, where the poor girl has only a paper dress to wear in the snow and the other girl is bundled up in furs.

An unusual aspect of this story is the opening, in which we learn that the king remarried shortly after his wife's death, not so that his daughter could have a mother, but instead because the woman was rich. The king is therefore responsible for his daughter's ill treatment, which spawns the chain of events. In Shakespeare's play *Hamlet*, the pivotal event that springs the play's action is the remarriage of Hamlet's mother two months after her husband's death.

Another unusual twist to this story is the kind cobbler, who reverses the curses set upon the second sister. He provides the second daughter with magical cures obtained from a hermit. (A hermit is a person who lives alone and is often associated with spirituality.) Usually a severe punishment ends the story for the selfish person. This variant offers the possibility that, with help, even a mean-spirited person can change. This girl is not left with the visible riches of her sister, but she has the possibility of a self-fulfilling life.

Shoes are sometimes used by psychologists as female symbols. Folklorist Alan Dundes commented, "If the old woman who lived in a shoe had known what to do — about birth control — she would not have had so many children." Jungian psychologists point out that men have an anima (a feminine side), and women have an animus (a masculine side). How this develops affects the way the person deals with the world. This cobbler, working with shoes, appears to have developed his anima in a positive way and, consequently, chooses to help this disagreeable girl and is rewarded. He offers a counterpoint to the king, who is not in touch with his anima, having married an ugly old woman for her money.

Motifs

Q2.1.1Ba - Kind and unkind girls following the River subtype. The Three Heads

S31 - cruel stepmother

H1245 - heroine has poor food for journey, other girlgood provisions

N825.2 - encounter with old man

Q42 - generosity

Q42.1.1 - child divides last loaf with fairy (witch, etc.)

Q41 - general politeness

W31 - obedience

J150 - other means of acquiring knowledge [advice taken]

B822 - magic wand or stick

D1610.5 - magic speaking head[disembodied]

H1192 - combing hair

W27 - gratitude

D1860 - magic beautification

D2150 - miscellaneous magic manifestations

L162 - favorable marriage

J2415 - foolish imitation of lucky man

W158 - inhospitality

Q45 - inhospitality punished

W10 - kindness [cobbler]

Q280 - unkindness punished

21. The Green Lady

Once upon a time, there was man who had two daughters. Now one of these girls was a steady, decent girl, and the other was stuck-up and conceited, but the father liked the latter best, and she had the most to eat and the best clothes to wear. One day, the nice girl said to her father, "Father, give me a cake and a bottle of ale, and let me go and seek my fortune."

So the father gave her a cake and a bottle of ale, and she went out to seek her fortune. After she had walked a weary while through the wood, she sat down by a tree to rest and to eat her cake and drink her ale. While she was eating, a little old man came by, and he said, "Little girl, little girl, what are you doing under my tree?"

She said, "I am going to seek my fortune, sir; I am very tired and hungry, and I am eating my dinner."

The old man said, "Little girl, little girl, give me some dinner, too."

She said, "I have only a cake and a bottle of ale; if you would like to have some of that, you may."

The old man said he would, so he sat down and they ate the cake and drank the ale. Then the old man said, "I will tell you where to seek your fortune. Go on further into the wood, until you come to a little old cottage, where the Green Lady lives. Knock at the door, and when she opens it, tell her you've come to seek service. She will take you in; mind you, be a good girl and do all she tells you to do, and you'll come to no harm."

So the little girl thanked him kindly and went on her way. Soon she came to the little cottage in the wood, and she knocked at the door. The door was opened by a pretty Green Lady, who said, "Little girl, little girl, what do you want?"

"I've come to seek service, ma'am," said the little girl.

"What can you do?" asked the Green Lady.

"I can bake and I can brew, and about the house, most things I can do," said the little girl.

"Then come in," said the Green Lady, and she took her into the kitchen. "Now," said she, "you must be a very good girl. Sweep the house well. Make the dust fly, and mind you don't look through the keyhole, or harm will befall you."

The little girl swept the house and made the dust fly.

Then the Green Lady said, "Now go to the well, and bring in a pail of nice clean water to cook the supper in. If the water isn't clean, change it and change it till it is."

Then the little girl took a pail and went to the well. The first pail she drew, the water was muddy and dirty, so she threw it away. The next pail of water was a little clearer, but there was a silver fish in it.

The fish said, "Little girl, little girl, wash me and comb me, and lay me down softly."

So she washed it and combed it and laid it down softly. Then she drew another pailful. The water was a little clearer, but there was a gold fish in it.

The fish said, "Little girl, little girl, wash me and comb me, and lay me down softly."

So she washed it and combed it and laid it down softly. Then she drew another pailful. There was clear water, but there was still another fish who said the same thing as the others, so she washed this one, too, combed it, and laid it down softly. Then she drew another pailful, and this was quite fresh and clear.

Then the three fish raised their heads and said:

"They who eat the fairies' food
    In the churchyard soon shall dwell.
    Drink the water of this well,
    And all things for thee shall be good.
    Be but honest, bold and true,
    So shall good fortune come to you."

Then the little girl hastened to the house, swept up the kitchen, and made the dust fly quickly, for she thought she would surely be scolded for being away so long, and she was hungry, too. The Green Lady then showed her how to cook the supper and told her she could take some bread and milk for herself afterward. But the girl said she would rather have a drink of water and some of her own cake, although she had only a few crumbs in her pocket. Then the Green Lady went into the parlor, and the little girl lay down by the fire. She was thinking about what the fish had said, and she wondered why the Green Lady had told her not to look through the keyhole. She thought there could not be any harm in doing this, so she looked, and what should she see but the Green Lady dancing with a bogey! She was so surprised that she said,

"Oh! What can I see? The Green Lady is dancing with a bogey."

The Green Lady rushed out of the room and said, "What did you see?"

The little girl replied, "Nothing did I see, nothing did I spy, that is what I will say, till the day I die."

Then the Green Lady went away, and the little girl again looked through the keyhole. Again she said, "Oh! What can I see? The Green Lady is dancing with a bogey."

The Green Lady rushed out. "Little girl, little girl, what did you see?"

The girl said, "Nothing did I see, nothing did I spy, that is what I will say, till the day I die."

This happened a third time, and then the Green Lady said, "Now you shall see no more," and she blinded the little girl's eyes. "But," said the Green Lady, "because you have been a good girl and made the dust fly, I will give you your wages and you shall go home."

So she gave her a bag of money and a bundle of clothes and sent her away. The little girl stumbled along the path in the dark, and presently she bumped into the well. Now, there was a fine young man sitting on the edge of the well, and he told her that he had been sent by the fish of the well to see her home, and that he would carry her bags and bundles. He told her to bathe her eyes in the well. When she did this, she could see as well as ever. So the young man and the little girl went along together, until they arrived at her father's cottage. When the bag was opened, there were all sorts of money in it, and when the bundle was opened, there were all sorts of fine clothes in it. And the little girl married the young man, and they lived happily ever after.

Now, when the other girl saw all the fine things her sister had got, she came to her father and said, "Father, give me a cake and a bottle of ale, and let me seek my fortune."

Her father gave her a cake and a bottle of ale, and the same things happened to her as to her sister. But when the old man asked her for some dinner, she said, "I have barely enough for myself," and she didn't give him any. And when she was at the Green Lady's house, she didn't make the dust fly, and the Green Lady was cross with her. When she went to the well and the fish got into her pails of water, she said the fish were wet, sloppy things, and she wasn't going to mess her hands or dirty her clean frock with them, and she threw them back roughly into the well. She said she wasn't going to drink nasty cold water for her supper; she wanted nice bread and milk. And when the Green Lady put her eyes out for looking through the keyhole, she didn't get a bag of money and a bundle of clothes or her wages, because she hadn't made the dust fly, and so she had no one to help her and take her home. She wandered about, not knowing where she was going, and no one knows where she was buried or what became of her.

What goes around, comes around.

U.S. folk saying

Story Notes:

This story has much in common with the previous story, "The Three Heads of the Well," (page 86). This time, however, it is the father who prefers the conceited daughter. The girls meet fish at the well, who ask the same tasks as the three heads of the well in the previous tale, also from England.

The fish chant:

"They who eat the fairies' food

In the churchyard soon shall dwell,"

warning the girl that if she eats anything in fairyland, it could result in death. In the Greek myth *Demeter and Persephone,* Persophenoe eats several persimmon seeds and, as a result, has to return to live in the underworld part of the year.

This story adds a titillating, dangerous theme: the Green Lady is dancing with a bogeyman, which the girl sees through a keyhole. This looking at something she has been forbidden to see and denying that she has done so is reminiscent of the story of *Bluebeard,* in which the girl uses the key to open a forbidden door and sees a frightening sight.

Motifs:

Q2.1.1B - Kind and unkind girls following the river subtype. Heads in the Well group.

N825.2 - encounter with old man

Q42.1.1 - child divides last loaf with fairy (witch, etc)

W11 - generosity

H1192 - combing hair

F200 - fairies [green lady]

F210 - fairyland

C611 - forbidden chamber

C300 - looking tabu ["don't look through the keyhole"]

F378.0.1 - mortal expelled from fairyland for breaking tabu

W126 - disobedience

Q325 - disobedience punished

Q62 - reward for ability to keep secrets

F340 - gifts from fairies

D1658.3.1 - being encountered assists in the journey

W151 - greed

J2415 - foolish imitation of lucky man

W198 - unkindness

Q280 - unkindness punished

Q580 - punishment fitted to crime [blinded]

22. The Two Stepsisters

NORWAY

Once upon a time there were a husband and wife who each had a daughter by a former marriage. While the woman's daughter was dull and lazy, the man's daughter was spirited and industrious; nonetheless, she could never do anything to her stepmother's liking.

Now it happened one day that the two girls were to go out and spin by the side of the well.

"You're always so quick and sharp," said the woman's daughter, "but I'm not afraid to have a spinning match with you."

They agreed that the one whose thread first snapped would have to go down the well. So they both began to spin, but suddenly the man's daughter's thread broke, so she had to go down the well. But when she got to the bottom, she found herself in a green meadow, and she had not hurt herself at all! She walked on a bit, until she came to a hedge, which she had to climb over.

"Ah, don't step hard on me, please don't, and I'll help you another time, that I will," said the hedge.

Then the Lassie made herself as light as she could and went over the hedge so carefully that she scarce touched a twig.

She went a bit further, till she came to a cow, which had a milking pail on her horns. "Ah, pray be so good as to milk me," said the cow. "I'm so full of milk. Drink as much as you please, and throw the rest over my hooves, and see if I don't help you some-day."

So the man's daughter did as the cow asked. As soon as she touched the teats, milk spouted out into the pail. Then she drank till her thirst was quenched, and the rest she threw over the cow's hooves, and the milking pail she hung on the cow's horns again.

She went further, and a woolly white sheep walked over to her. It had thick long wool that hung down and dragged after it on the ground. On one of the horns hung a great pair of shears.

"Ah, please clip off my wool," said the sheep, "for with all this wool I get caught on bushes and trees, and besides, it's so warm, I'm suffocating. Take as much of the fleece as you please, and twist the rest round my neck. And see if I don't help you someday."

Yes; she was willing enough, so the sheep lay down on her lap and kept quite still, and she clipped him so neatly there wasn't a scratch on his skin. Then she took a bundle of wool, and the rest she twisted around the sheep's neck.

She walked a little further and came to an apple tree, which was so covered with apples that all its branches were bowed to the ground. Leaning against the stem was a slender pole.

"Ah, please be so good as to pluck my apples," said the tree, "so that my branches can straighten up. You may eat as many as you please; then lay the rest around my root and see if I don't help you someday."

Yes; she plucked all she could reach with her hands, and then she took the pole and carefully knocked down the apples higher up on the tree's limbs. Afterward she ate her fill, and the rest of the apples she laid neatly around the root.

She continued walking until she saw a large farmhouse. The girl knocked on the door and asked, "Do you have some work that I could do for you?" Now, in this house lived the old hag of the trolls and her daughter, and when she opened the door, the old hag said, "Oh! You might as well leave. We have had many girls come to work for us, but none of them was any help at all."

The girl asked again, "Please, could I work for you on a trial basis? I won't ask for anything until you decide if you like my services."

"Very well," said the old hag. "Take this sieve and bring it back filled with water."

The girl thought it was very strange that the old hag thought she could carry water in a sieve. Why, it would all drain out. But when she got to the well, little birds in the trees began to sing, "Daub in clay. Stuff in straw." That sounded like a good idea, and when she did that, she was able to fill the sieve with water and bring it back.

"You have been helped!" the old hag screamed. "Now, go to the barn and clean it out. And while you are there, milk the cows." When the girl went inside the barn she found a pitchfork that was so long and heavy she could barely lift it. The little birds outside began to sing. "Use the broom. Sweep a little, and the rest will follow." So she swept with the broom, and huge piles of dung and dirt flew out the barn door. Before long, the barn was clean.

Now she tried to milk the cows, but they jumped and kicked and she could not get close to them. She heard the birds singing, "A little drop, a tiny sup. Give it to the birds to drink it up." So she carefully got close enough to get one tiny drop of milk, which she gave to a little bird. Then all the cows stood still and let her milk them. They neither kicked nor frisked; they did not even lift a leg.

When the old hag saw her coming, she screamed, "You have been helped!"

Now the old hag gave her some black wool and told her to wash it until it was white. The girl did not know what to say; she had never seen or heard of anyone who could wash black wool white. She took the wool and went back to the well. The birds sang, "Dip the wool in the tub. It will turn white. No need to scrub." She did, and when she pulled it out, it was white!

"Well, I never!" said the old troll when the girl came in with the wool. "It's no good keeping you. You can do anything. I'll give you your wages, and you can be off."

The troll showed her three boxes — one red, one green, and one blue — and said, "Choose one." The girl did not know which one to take. From outside she could hear the birds. "Don't take the red or the green. Take the blue — we have seen!" So she chose the blue box, and the old hag said, "Oh! I'll make you pay for that!"

The girl ran out the door and down the path, but when she got to the apple tree, she could hear the old hag and her daughter running after her. She was frightened.

"Come here, Lassie," said the apple tree. "Hide under my branches." The girl had scarcely hidden herself when the troll and her daughter came up to the tree and asked, "Have you seen a Lassie pass this way?"

"Yes, yes," said the apple tree. "But she was going so fast you would never be able to catch up with her."

So the troll and her daughter turned back and went home again.

The girl thanked the tree and ran on, but after a while, she heard the old troll and her daughter coming after her again. They had decided to try to catch up with the girl after all. Just then she saw the sheep, who said, "Hide under my fleece, and they will not see you." She had just hidden herself when the troll was there and asked, "Sheep, have you seen a Lassie passing this way?"

"Oh, yes," said the sheep. "A long time ago. She was running so fast you will never be able to catch up with her."

So the old witch and her daughter turned around and went home.

But when the girl came to the place where she had milked the cow, she heard the troll and her daughter again. Just then the cow appeared and said, "Lassie, hide under my udder."

It was not long before the old hag was there. "Cow, have you seen a Lassie pass this way?"

"Yes. Why yes. But that was a very long time ago. You could not possibly catch up with her."

The girl thanked the cow and ran as fast as she could. But just as she was about to climb over the hedge, she heard the troll coming again. "Climb under my branches, Lassie. If they catch you they will take the blue box and tear you to pieces."

The girl quickly climbed under the twigs of the hedge.

Soon she heard the old troll asking, "Hedge, have you seen a Lassie pass this way?"

"No, I have not seen any Lassie," answered the hedge, and was as smooth tongued as if he had melted butter in his mouth. And as he spoke, he spread himself out and made himself big and tall. The old troll turned around and went home.

When the girl finally got home, her stepmother and stepsister were very angry to see her and made her go out to the pigsty. "That will be your new home," they told her. First, the girl scrubbed it and cleaned it, and then she decided to open the blue box to see what she had been given for her wages. As soon as she opened it, she saw gold and silver and lovely things that poured out of the box and filled the pigsty until it was as grand as a king's palace. When her stepmother saw this, she was astonished. "Where did you get that?" she asked.

"Oh," said the Lassie, "these are my wages. I worked for a family at the bottom of the well."

Well, the woman's daughter made up her mind that she would go down the well. And like her sister, she landed in a lovely green meadow. When she had walked a bit, she saw she had to cross over a hedge.

"Step carefully over me, Lassie, and I'll help you again."

"Oh!" she thought, "what do I care about a bundle of twigs?" and she tramped and stamped right over the hedge.

A little further on she came to the cow. "Be so good as to milk me, Lassie, and I will help you again. Drink as much as you please and throw the rest over my hooves."

She drank till she could drink no more, and there was not any milk left to throw over the cow's hooves. And as for the pail, she tossed it down the hill, and she walked on.

After a while, she came to the sheep. "Oh, be so good as to clip me, Lassie. Take as much wool as you want, but twist the rest around my neck."

Well, she did that, but so carelessly that she cut the sheep many times. And as for the wool, she carried it all away with her.

A little while later she came to the apple tree. "Be so good as to pluck the apples off me. You can eat as many as you like, but lay the rest neatly around my root, and I will help you again."

Well, she picked those nearest to her and thrashed with the pole, breaking a few branches. Then she ate until she was full as full could be and went on her way.

A good bit further on she came to the farm where the old troll lived. "I am looking for a place to work," she told the troll. "No," said the old hag, "we don't want any more helpers. They are either worth nothing or else too clever." The girl agreed to work for nothing, on a trial basis, and the first thing they asked her to do was to bring back water in a sieve. The birds sang, "Daub in clay, put in straw," but the girl was struggling to make the water stop pouring out of the sieve, and their singing irritated her. She used the clay to pelt the birds until they flew away. When she returned with an empty sieve, you can imagine how that old troll scolded her.

Next she was sent to clean the barn. The birds told her to use the broomstick, but all she did with that broomstick was to throw it at those noisy birds! Then she tried to milk the cows, but they kicked and pushed, and when she did get a little milk, they kicked it over. The birds sang again, "A little drop, and a tiny sup, for the little birds to drink it up." But she didn't listen, she was so busy screaming and chasing the cows. When she went back to the house, there were hard blows as well as hard words from the old troll. Then she was told, "Now, take this black wool and wash it until it is white."

She did this no better than the other tasks, and the old hag decided to send her on her way. She pulled out three boxes, one red, one green, and one  blue. "Which box do you want?" she asked. The birds outside were singing, "Don't take the red, don't take the green. Take the blue, we have seen." But she did not care a pin for what the birds sang, but took the red, which caught her eye most. And so she set out on her road home, and she went along quietly and easily enough; no one came after her.

When she got home, her mother was ready to jump with joy. They went at once to open the box in the barn, thinking it was much larger than the pigsty, and soon the entire barn would be covered with gold and silver and other lovely things. But when they opened the red box, out jumped frogs and toads and snakes.

Do good and don't look back.

Dutch proverb

Story Notes:

Folklorist often refer to Tale Type 480 as "The Spinning Women at the Well," as this is a well-known variation.

In Norwegian folk tales, trolls are strange-looking little people, usually malevolent. It is interesting to see the same function played by King Frost, a witch, a sparrow, the Madonna, and a troll in these variations of Tale Type 480 collected from around the world.

Motifs:

Q2.1.2Ab - kind and unkind girls encounters en route - fall into the well

G204 - girl in service of witch

N777.4 - loser of spinning contest must go down into well

D1658.2.4 - fence or hedge asks to be treated gently

B394.1 - cow [with pail on horns] grateful for being milked

B395. - sheep grateful for being sheared

G304 - troll

B400. - helpful domestic animals

H1023.2 - Task: carrying water in a sieve, sieve filled with moss, leaves, etc.

D1658.3.4 - grateful objects [or beings] help fugitive

H1023.6 - washing black wool white, or vice versa

B270 - speaking animals

B216 - knowledge of animal languages

B560. - animals advise men

B469.1 - helpful sparrows

W10 - kindness

L210. - heroine offered choice between containers

B562.3 - helper advises which reward to choose

Q111. - riches as reward; gold, silver, money, etc.

W198 - unkindness

Q280 - unkindness punished

Q66 - humility rewarded

Q331 - pride punished

23. The Talking Eggs

CREOLE (LOUISIANA), UNITED STATES

There was once a lady who had two daughters. They were called Rose and Blanche. Rose was bad and Blanche was good. But the mother liked Rose better because she was her very picture. She made Blanche do all the work, while Rose was seated in her rocking chair.

One day, the mother sent Blanche to the well to get some water in a bucket. When Blanche arrived at the well, she saw an old woman, who said to her, "Pray, my little one, give me some water. I am very thirsty."

"Yes, Auntie," said Blanche, "here is some water." And Blanche rinsed her bucket and gave the old woman good fresh water to drink.

"Thank you, my child. You are a good girl," the old woman said.

A few days later, the mother was so mean to Blanche that she ran away into the woods. She cried and did not know where to go. Then she saw the same old woman walking in front of her.

"Ah, my child, why are you crying?" the old woman asked. "What hurts you?"

"Oh, Aunt, Mamma has beaten me, and I am afraid to return to the cabin."

"Well, my child, come with me. I will give you supper and a bed. But you must promise not to laugh at anything you see." She took Blanche's hand, and they began to walk in the woods.

As they advanced, the bushes of thorns opened before them and closed behind their backs. A little further on, Blanche saw two axes that were fighting. She found that very strange and comical but said nothing. They walked further, and behold! It was two arms that were fighting. A little further two legs. Then she saw two heads that were fighting, and they said, "Blanche, good morning, my child."

At last they arrived at a cabin, and the old woman said, "Make some fire, my child, to cook the supper." The old woman sat down near the fireplace and took off her head. She placed it on her knees and began to delouse her hair.

Blanche found this very strange, but she said nothing. After a while, the old woman put her head back in its place and gave Blanche a large bone to put on the fire for their supper. Blanche put the bone in the pot. Lo! In a moment, the pot was full of good meat.

The old woman gave Blanche a grain of rice to pound with the pestle, and immediately the mortar became full of rice. After they had eaten their supper, the old woman said to Blanche, "Pray, my child, scratch my back."

Blanche scratched her back, but her hand was all cut because the old woman's back was covered with broken glass. When she saw that Blanche's hands were bleeding, the old woman blew on them, and the cuts disappeared.

When Blanche got up the next morning, the old woman said to her, "You must go home now. You are a good girl, and I want to give you a present. Go to the chicken house. All the eggs that say 'Take me,' you can take. All the eggs that say 'Do not take me' you must not take. When you are on the road, throw the eggs behind your back and break them."

Blanche did as she had been told, and when she broke the eggs, many pretty things came out - diamonds, gold, a beautiful carriage, lovely dresses. When she arrived at her mother's, the house was filled with these fine things, and her mother was therefore very glad to see her.

The next day, the mother said to Rose, "You must go to the woods to look for this same old woman. You must have fine dresses like Blanche."

Rose went to the woods, and she found the old woman, who told her to come to her cabin. But when she saw the axes, the arms, the legs, and the heads fighting and the old woman taking off her head to delouse herself, she began to laugh and ridicule everything she saw. Therefore the old woman said, "Ah, my child, you are not a good girl."

The next day, she said to Rose, "I don't want to send you back with nothing. Go to the chicken house and take the eggs that say 'take me.'" Rose went to the chicken house. Some eggs began to say "Take me," and others, "Don't take me." Rose was so bad that she said, "Ah, yes, you say 'Don't take me,' but you are precisely what I want." And Rose took all the eggs that said "Don't take me."

As she walked, she broke the eggs, and out came snakes, toads, and frogs, which began to run after her. Rose ran and shrieked. She arrived at her mother's so tired that she was not able to speak. When her mother saw all the beasts, she was so angry that she sent Rose away.

 When one door closes, another opens.

Spanish proverb

Story Notes:

Many themes and motifs in African tales can be found in stories collected in southern areas of the United States. *The Talking Eggs,* collected from the Cajun culture, has French roots. An African variant with talking eggs as a key motif was collected in the French language in Africa, see page 68. See also "The String of Beads," page 60, where the girl helps a woman with wounds.

Motifs:

Q2. - Kind and unkind

Q2.1.2Eb - snakes besiege unkind girl

S10 - cruel parents

H935 - old woman or witch gives rewards

E783 - disembodied body members

F990. - inanimate objects act as if living-objects and go journeying

G466 - lousing a person

G219.3 - scratching or washing person's back that is covered with nails, broken glass, etc.

F950 - marvelous cures

D1610.3. - magic speaking objects; "Take me", "Don't take me"

B562.3 - helper advises which reward to choose

D1470 - magic object as provider [of wealth]

J2400 - foolish imitation

W198 - unkindness

Q280 - unkindness punished

24. Diamonds and Toads

FRANCE

There was once upon a time a widow who had two daughters. The elder was like her mother, who was disagreeable and proud. The younger daughter resembled her father and was known for her courtesy and sweetness. As people naturally love their own likeness, this mother doted on her elder daughter and had a horrible aversion for the younger. She made her eat in the kitchen and work continually.

Among other things, this poor child was forced twice a day to bring home a pitcher of water from a well nearly a mile and a half from the house. One day, as she was at this fountain, a poor woman came up to her and begged, "Please, I am so thirsty. Will you get me a drink of water?"

"Aye, with all my heart, Goody," said this pretty little girl. She rinsed the pitcher and filled it with water from the clearest place of the fountain. Then she held the pitcher and poured from it, so that the old woman could easily drink the water.

The good woman, refreshed, said to her, "You are so very kind, my dear. I would like to give you a gift." For, you see, this was a fairy, who had taken the form of a poor country woman to see how far the civility and good manners of this pretty girl would go. "I will give you for your gift," continued the fairy, "that at every word you speak, there shall come out of your mouth either a flower or a jewel."

When the girl came home, her mother scolded her for staying so long at the fountain.

"I beg your pardon, mamma," said the poor girl, "for not making more haste."

When she spoke, there came out of her mouth two roses, two pearls, and two diamonds.

"What is it I see there?" said her mother, quite astonished. "I think I saw pearls and diamonds coming out of the girl's mouth! How happens this, Child?" This was the first time she had ever called her Child.

The girl told her what had happened at the well, and as she spoke, diamonds and roses fell from her mouth.

"In good faith," cried the mother, "I must send my dear child to the well. Come hither, Fanny. Look what has fallen from your sister's mouth. I want you to have the same gift! All you have to do is go to the fountain and give a drink of water to a poor woman."

"It would be a very fine sight indeed," said Fanny, "to see me walk to the well and draw water."

"You shall go!" said the mother, "and this minute."

So carrying the best silver tankard in the house, away she went, grumbling all the way to the well. She was no sooner at the fountain than she saw coming out of the wood a gloriously dressed lady.

"My dear," the woman said, "would you please give me a drink of water?" This was, as you may have guessed, the very fairy who had appeared to her sister, but had now taken the appearance of a princess to see how far this girl's rudeness would go.

"Am I come hither to serve you with water? I suppose the silver tankard was brought purely for your ladyship, was it? However, you may drink out of it, if you have a fancy."

"You are not very mannerly," answered the fairy. "Well, then, since you are so rude, at every word you speak there shall come out of your mouth a snake or a toad."

The girl returned home, and as soon as her mother saw her coming, she cried out, "Well, Daughter?"

"Well, Mother?" answered the girl in a nasty tone of voice, and out from her mouth came two vipers and two toads.

"Oh mercy!" cried the mother. "What do I see? Oh! It is that wretch your sister who has caused this, and she shall pay for it," and she ran to give the girl a beating. But the girl saw her coming and fled to hide in the forest.

The king's son, on his return from hunting, happened upon her and asked, "Why are you alone in the forest? And why are you crying?"

"Alas, sir, my mamma has turned me out of doors."

The king's son, who saw five or six pearls and as many diamonds come out of her mouth, asked her to tell him how and why this was happening. She told him the whole story and as he looked at her and listened to her tale, the king's son fell in love. He took her to the palace, and when she was certain she wished to marry him, they told the king, who agreed to the match.

As for her sister, she became more and more hateful until even her own mother could not abide living with her and made her leave. The girl wandered about in the woods and probably died there in the forest.

> ❧ *Opportunities, like eggs, come one at a time.* ❧
>
> U.S. folk saying

Story Notes:

This tale appeared in Perrault's publication *Contes de Ma Mere L'Oye* (1695), under the title "Les Fees." The first English translation appeared in 1729 in *Histories or Tales of Past Times.* Today this tale is usually known as "Diamonds and Toads."

A version of the tale appears in the fourth part of *Il Pentamerone* (1634). In the story of the two cakes, "Le Doie Pizzele," the two girls are cousins. The fair one, Marziella, goes to the well to fetch water, taking a cake with her. When she shares her cake with an old woman, she is blessed with three gifts: the breath of roses and jasmine, the footprints of violets and lilies, and the more practical ability to comb pearls and garnets from her hair. (motif Q149.1 - flowers springing from footprints; motif D 1454.1 - gold, pearls, etc. falling from hair) The mean cousin, Puccia, attempts to imitate her but tells the old woman that only fools give away their provisions. Consequently, she returns, foaming at the mouth like a mule, making thistles grow where she steps, and producing lice whenever she combs her hair.

Motifs:

Q2.1.1Aa - kind and unkind girls; following the river subtype; drink of water
     Group; Toads and Diamonds

F234.2 - encounter with fairy [old lady]

D1454.2.1 - flowers fall from mouth

D1454.2 - treasure [jewels] fall from mouth

Q111 - riches as reward

J2400 - foolish imitation

M431.2 - toads fall from mouth

M431.2.1 - curse: reptiles fall from mouth

Q40 - kindness rewarded

Q280 - unkindness punished

---

25. The Girls and the Hogs

MUSHKOGEAN, AMERICAN INDIAN

An old woman and her granddaughter were living in a certain place. One time, the old woman said to the girl, "Go and hunt for some hogs," so the girl took some bread made of chaff and started out.

After she had gone along for some time, she met two old women, who said, "What have you got?"

"Chaff bread," she answered. "Do you want some?"

"No. Where are you going?"

"I am out hunting hogs."

Then the old women said, "We will help you find the hogs," and they drove the hogs to the place where the girl was waiting. Then the girl started along home, driving her hogs. By and by, however, one ran away and she went after it, chasing it round and round. At last she got tired and coughed. At the second cough, she coughed a nickel out of her mouth.

By and by the same hog again ran off. Again she ran after it; and again she got tired and coughed. She coughed up a dime. The same thing happened again; this time she coughed up a quarter. She had now reached home, and she went on coughing — coughing up nickels, dimes, and quarters — until she had a whole box full of money. The white people saw the things this girl had coughed up, and they liked them and got them from her.

Another woman was jealous, and she sent her daughter after hogs, providing her with a sack full of biscuits. By and by that girl came to the two old women. They said, "What do you have there?"

She said, "Biscuits."

"May we have some?" they asked her.

"No."

Then they asked, "Where are you going?"

"I am out hunting hogs."

The old women told her they would get the hogs for her, and they did. The girl started for home with the hogs, and on the way she began to

cough, but she coughed up a frog. She coughed again and spit up another frog. She kept on doing this when she got home, and after a time she died.

 Virtue passes current all over the world.

Greek proverb

Story Notes:

This story is from the Mushkogean Indians (a branch of the Algonquin woodland Indians), who are the source of the name of the state of Michigan. The first two syllables mean "great," and the second two, "water." The great lake on Michigan's left border is, of course, Lake Michigan.

To "cough up money" — which the girl does in this story — is a folk expression like "not to be sneezed at," where bodily functions transpose to folk speech.

Motifs:

Q2.1-kind and unkind girls

Q2.1.2C encounters en route subtype pursuit Form

H935-old woman or witch encountered who gives rewards

W11 - generosity

D1454.2. - gems, gold [money], etc. fall from mouth

Q280 - unkindness punished

M431.2 - frogs or toads fall from mouth

26. House of Cats

MILAN, ITALY

Long, long ago, as far back as the time when animals spoke, a community of cats lived in a deserted house they had taken possession of not far from a large town. They had everything they could possibly desire for their comfort. The old people of the town related how they had heard their parents speak of a time when the whole country was so overrun with rats and mice that there was not so much as a grain of corn nor an ear of maize to be gathered in the fields, and it might be out of gratitude to the cats who had rid the country of these plagues that their descendants were allowed to live in peace. No one knows where they got the money to pay for everything, for all this happened so very long ago. But one thing is certain: they were rich enough to keep a servant, for though they lived very happily together and did not scratch or fight more than human beings would have done, they were not clever enough to do the housework themselves and preferred at all events to have someone to cook their meat, which they would have scorned to eat raw. Since they were very difficult to please about the housework and most women quickly tired of living with only cats for companions, they never kept a servant long. It had become a saying in the town, when a girl or woman found herself reduced to her last penny, "I will go and live with the cats," and many a poor woman actually did.

Now Lizina was not happy at home, for her mother, a widow, was much fonder of her older sister. Lizina was treated badly and often did not have enough to eat, while her older sister could have anything she desired. If Lizina dared to complain, she was certain to receive a beating.

At last a day came when she was at the end of her courage and patience. She said, "As you hate me so much, you will be glad to be rid of me, so I am going to go and live with the cats!"

"Be off with you!" cried her mother, seizing an old broom handle from behind the door. Poor Lizina did not wait to be told twice; she ran off at once and did not stop until she reached the door of the cats' house. As it happened, their cook had left them that very morning. Lizina, therefore, was warmly welcomed, and she set to work at once to prepare the dinner, not without many misgivings as to the tastes of the cats and whether she would be able to satisfy them.

Going to and fro about her work, she found herself frequently hindered by a constant succession of cats who appeared one after another in the kitchen to inspect the new servant. She had one by her feet, another perched on the back of her chair while she peeled vegetables, a third on the table beside her, and five or six others prowling about among the pots and pans on the shelves against the wall. The air resounded with their purring, which meant that they were pleased with their new maid, but Lizina had not yet learned to understand their language. As she was a good, kindhearted girl, however, she set to work, and in between chores she picked up the little kittens that tumbled about on the floor, patched up quarrels, and nursed on her lap a big tabby, the oldest of the community, which had a lame paw. All these kindnesses could hardly fail to make a favorable impression on the cats, and they liked her even more as time went on. Lizina kept the house clean, the meals well served, and the sick cats well cared for.

After a time the cats had a visit from an old cat, whom they called their father, who lived by himself in a barn at the top of the hill and came down from time to time to inspect the little colony. He too was much taken with Lizina, and when he asked, "Are you well served by this nice, black-eyed little person?" the cats answered with one voice, "Oh, yes, Father Gatto, we have never had so good a servant!"

At each of his visits the answer was always the same, but after a time the old cat, who was very observant, noticed that the girl looked   sad. Then one day he found her crying in the kitchen. "What is the matter, my child? Has anyone been unkind to you?" he asked. Lizina burst into tears and answered between her sobs, "No, oh, no! Everyone is very good to me, but I long for news from home, and I pine to see my mother and my sister."

Old Gatto, being a sensible old cat, understood her feelings. "You shall go home," he said, "and you shall not come back here unless it pleases you to do so. But first you must be rewarded for all your kind services to my children. Follow me down into the inner cellar, where you have not yet been, for I always keep it locked and carry the key away with me."

In the great vaulted cellar underneath the kitchen stood two enormous earthenware jars, one of which contained oil, the other a liquid shining like gold. "In which of these jars shall I dip you?" asked Father Gatto, with a grin that showed all his sharp white teeth, while his moustaches stood out straight on either side of his face. The little maid looked at the two jars from under her long dark lashes. "In the oil jar," she answered timidly, thinking to herself, "I could not ask to be bathed in gold." But Father Gatto replied, "No, no, you deserve better than that." And seizing her in his strong paws, he plunged her into the liquid gold. Wonder of wonders! When Lizina came out of the jar, she shone from head to foot like the sun in the heavens on a fine summer's day. Her pretty pink cheeks and long black hair kept their natural color, but otherwise she had become like a statue of pure gold. Father Gatto purred loudly with satisfaction. "Go home," he said, "and see your mother and sisters, but listen carefully to what I tell you. If you hear the cock crow, turn toward it. If you hear a donkey bray, you must remember to look the other way."

The little maid gratefully kissed the white paw of the old cat and set off for home. Just as she neared her mother's house, the cock crowed, so she quickly turned toward it. Immediately a beautiful golden star appeared on her forehead, crowning her glossy black hair. At the same time, the donkey began to bray, but she remembered not to look over the fence into the field where the donkey was feeding. Instead she looked the other way.

Her mother and sister, who were in front of their house, uttered cries of admiration and astonishment when they saw her. Their cries became still louder when Lizina took her handkerchief from her pocket and found it filled with gold.

For some days the mother and her two daughters lived very happily together, for Lizina had given them everything she had brought away except her golden clothing, for that would not come off, in spite of all the efforts of her sister, who was madly jealous about Lizina's good fortune. The golden star, too, could not be removed from her forehead. But all the gold pieces had found their way to her mother and sister.

One day Peppina, the older girl, said, "I will go now and see what I can get out of the cats."

The cats in the colony had not yet taken another servant, for they knew they could never get one to replace Lizina, whose loss they had not yet ceased to mourn. When they heard that Peppina was her sister, they all ran to meet her. "She does not appear the least like her," the kittens whispered among themselves. "Hush. Be quiet!" the older cats said. "All servants cannot be pretty."

However, decidedly she was not at all like Lizina. Even the most reasonable and open-minded of the cats soon acknowledged that. The very first day she shut the kitchen door in the face of the tomcats, who used to enjoy watching Lizina at her work, and a young and mischievous cat who jumped in by the open kitchen window and lighted on the table got such a blow with the rolling pin that he squalled for an hour.

With every day that passed, the household became more and more aware of its misfortune. The work was as badly done as the servant was surly and disagreeable. In the corners of the rooms heaps of dust collected. Spider webs hung from the ceilings and in front of the windowpanes. The beds were hardly ever made, and the feather beds, so beloved by the old and feeble cats, had never once been shaken since Lizina left the house. At Father Gatto's next visit, he found the whole colony in a state of uproar. "Caesar has one paw so badly swollen that it looks as if it were broken," they told him. "Peppina kicked him with her wooden shoes. Hector has an abscess in his back where a wooden chair hit him, and Agrippina's three little kittens have died of hunger beside their mother, because Peppina forgot them in their basket up in the attic. There is no putting up with the creature. Do send her away, Father Gatto! Lizina herself would not be angry with us, she must know very well what her sister is like."

"Come here," said Father Gatto, in his most severe tones, to Peppina. He took her down into the cellar and showed her the same two great jars that he had shown Lizina. "In which of these shall I dip you?" he asked, and she made haste to answer, "In the liquid gold," for she was no more modest than she was good and kind.

Father Gatto's yellow eyes darted fire. "You do not deserve that," he uttered, in a voice like thunder, and seizing her, he flung her into the jar of oil. When she came to the surface, the cat seized her again and rolled her in the ashes on the floor. She was dirty and disgusting as she went out the door. Father Gatto said, "Begone. If you hear a donkey braying, you might as well look at it."

Stumbling and raging, Peppina set off for home. She was within sight of her house when she heard in the meadow on the right the voice of a donkey loudly braying. She turned her head toward it and at the same time put her hand up to her forehead, where, waving like a plume, was a donkey's tail. She ran home to her mother at the top of her speed, screaming with rage and despair.

It took Lizina two hours with a big basin of hot water and two cakes of soap to get rid of the layer of ashes. As for the donkey tail, it was impossible to get rid of that; it was as firmly fixed on her forehead as was the golden star on Lizina's.

This made their mother even more furious with Lizina. She beat her with the broom, then took her to the well and lowered her into it, leaving her at the bottom weeping and crying for help.

Before this happened, however, the king's son had passed the mother's house and seen Lizina sitting sewing in the parlor. After coming back two or three times, he had at last ventured to approach the window, and he and Lizina had agreed in whispered speech to marry.

When he came for the marriage, the mother wrapped Peppina in a large white veil. "This is a well-known custom for the way maidens leave their parent's homes," said the mother. She had fastened the donkey's tail round Peppina's head like a lock of hair under the veil. The prince was young and a little timid, so he made no objections and seated Peppina in the carriage beside him.

Their way led past the old house inhabited by the cats, who were all at the window, for the report had got about that the prince was going to marry the most beautiful maiden in the world, on whose forehead shone a golden star, and they knew that this could only be their adored Lizina. As the carriage slowly passed in front of the old house, they saw who was inside, and they began to sing:

"*Mew, mew, mew!*
Prince, look quick behind you!
In the well is fair Lizina,
And you've got nothing but Peppina."

When he heard this, the coachman, who understood the cat's language better than the prince, stopped his horses and asked, "Does your highness know what the cats are saying?"

The song broke forth again, louder than ever. With a turn of his hand, the prince threw back the veil and discovered the sullen face of Peppina, with the donkey's tail twisted round her head. "Ah, traitress!" he exclaimed, and he ordered the horses to be turned round. He was quivering with rage toward the old woman who had sought to deceive him. With his hand on the hilt of his sword, he demanded Lizina in so fierce and commanding a voice that the mother hastened to the well to draw her prisoner out. Lizina's clothing and her star shone so brilliantly that when the prince led her home to his palace, the whole palace was lit up. Next day they were married, and they lived happily ever after; and all the cats, headed by old Father Gatto, were present at the wedding.

 There is as much in knowing how not to do wrong
as there is in knowing how to do right.

U. S. folk saying

Story Notes:

Peppina is a nickname, derivative for the name Josephina.

In this story, a houseful of cats fulfills the role played in other variants by Mother Holle, the trolls, the sparrow, and the witch. Also, the more common "shower of pitch" is modi-fied: the bad girl is dipped in oil and rolled in ashes.

Italian Folktales, by Italo Calvino (N.Y.: Harcourt Brace, 1956) pp.446-448, includes a similar tale, "The Tale of the Cats," which he notes was collected in Maglie, Apulia, Italy.

Motifs:

Q2.1.1Ca -Kind and Unkind girls; following the river subtype; The House of
    Cats

W10 - kindness

L210 - modest choice

F545.2.1 - gold star on forehead

B560 - animals advise

Q111 - wealth (gold, silver, money, etc.) as reward

W197 - self-centeredness

Q280 - unkindness punished

Q321 - laziness punished

Q475.2 - shower of pitch

K1911 - substituted bride

B2166 - knowledge of animal languages

B135 - cat betrays substitution

L162 - marriage with prince or other favorable marriage

Q280 - unkindness punished

D1870 - magic hideousness

27. The Good Child and the Bad

SPANISH TALE FROM ZUNI, SOUTHWEST AMERICAN INDIAN

A Mexican girl wanted to marry Lei's son. She was a poor girl with only one calf and no cow.

Lei's son did not want to marry a poor girl.

One day, the poor girl's mother was hungry for meat and said, "Let us kill the calf." Then she said, "Take out the stomach. Wash it well in the creek." When the girl put it in the creek, it slipped out of her hands into the water. She took a stick to get it, but a catfish took away the stomach. The girl cried.

Then a man came out of a house with walls but no roof. The man was dressed nicely. He said to the girl, "What are you crying for?" She said, "I dropped the stomach, and the fish took it. My mother will whip me."

"Don't cry," said the man. "Go down to that house, and you will find a baby. Kill that baby. Take its stomach." The girl went and saw the baby. It was a nice baby with black hair and eyes. It laughed all the time; it did not cry. She said, "I don't want to kill that baby. My mother may whip me. I don't care." She left the house. Again, she met the man. That man was Yosh (a shamen). "Where is the stomach?" "I did not kill that baby." "All right! You go home. Your mother won't whip you."

As soon as the girl went into the house, everything was bright and light. She had four big stars on her forehead! "Who is that girl?" asked her mother.

"Mother, that's me."

The mother said, "I have no nice girl like that. You must be the girl of some rich people."

"No, Mother, I am your daughter. I went to wash the calf's stomach. It slipped down, and a fish took it. I cried. A man came out of a house. He told me to go to a house and to kill a baby. But I did not want to kill a baby. Then I met the same man again. He said, 'Go home. Your mother will not whip you.' The man told me that." The girl sat down.

People found out that the woman had a nice girl. When Lei's son learned of this, he wanted to marry the girl with the stars.

Another girl wanted to marry Lei's son. She said, "Mother, let's kill a calf." They killed one and took out its stomach. She went to wash it. It slipped into the water, and the fish took it. She cried. The man came and said, "Go to that house. You will find a baby. Kill it and take its stomach." So she went down and did what the man told her to do. Yosh met her. He said, "You go home now to your mother. Now you will look different."

Her mother opened the door. Her mother saw a long horn sticking out from the girl's forehead. "What is the matter with you?" asked her mother. Her mother sawed off the horn with a meat saw and put a cloth around her head. The girl with the stars also wore a cloth around her head. Lei's son made a mistake and married the girl with the horn.

The girl with the stars on her forehead married a poor man and was very happy. That's how Mexicans get rich. Rich men make mistakes, and pretty soon they are poor. If a poor man makes no mistakes, he will get rich. That's a Mexican story.

❧ *What you sow, you reap.* ❧
Turkish proverb

Story Notes:

This story was told in English by Nick from the Zuni nation and recorded in 1920 by E. C. Parsons. Nick said that he learned his stories while working in a sheep camp.

In this story, the second girl loses the meat she is washing in the creek. This motif of losing something in water is also in "Mother Holle" (page 34), when a spindle falls down inside a well; in "The Golden Axe," (page 16); and in "The String of Beads" (page 60), although in that story the girl consciously throws her necklace into the river on the advice of her friends. Psychologists suggest that water is a symbol for the unconscious, and losing something in water is a metaphor for not being in touch with oneself.

Other similar motifs appear in these tales — for example, the star on the forehead appears in "The House of Cats" and "The Bucket." The only other story with a baby as a key character is the Italian story "The Bucket," page 118.

Motifs:

Q2.1.2C - Kind and unkind girls encounters en route subtype with pursuit

N789.1 - river carries off an object the heroine pursues [animal intestines/
    stomach]

H580.1 - heroine is given enigmatic commands and must do the opposite

F545.2.1 - reward: golden star on forehead

J2400 - foolish imitation

C900 - punishment for breaking tabu [long horn on forehead]

D992.1 - disfigurement of head-animal horns

28. The Bucket

MILAN, ITALY

here was once a mother who had two daughters. One was bad, and the
other was very good. But the mother loved the bad one more than the
good one. She said one day to the bad one, "Go and draw a bucket of
water." The bad one did not want to go. The good daughter said, "I will go." She
went to draw the water, and the bucket fell down the well.

She said, "If I go home now without the bucket, who knows what my mother
will do to me?" So she climbed down the well and at the bottom found a narrow
passage with a door.

She knocked at the door, and a saint opened it. The girl asked, "Have you
found a cord and bucket?" The saint answered, "No, my child."

She walked on and found another door. She asked, "Have you found a cord and
bucket?" "No!" It was the devil. He answered her angrily because she was a good
girl.

She knocked at another door. "Have you found a cord and bucket?" It was the
Madonna, who replied, "Yes, my child. Would you do me a favor and stay here
while I am away? I have a little son. Give him his soup, sweep, and put the house

in order, and when I come home I will give you your bucket." Then she went away, and the good girl put the house in order and gave the child his broth. While she was sweeping, instead of finding dirt, she found coral and other beautiful things. She put these things aside to give to the Madonna when she returned.

When the Madonna came back, she asked, "Have you done all I told you to do?"

The good girl answered, "Yes, but I have kept some things here. I found them on the ground; they are not dirt."

"You may keep them for yourself. Now tell me, would you like a dress of calico, or one of silk?" The girl answered, "Calico." Instead of that, the Madonna gave her the silk one.

"Do you wish a brass thimble, or a silver one?"

"Brass."

"No, take the silver thimble. And here is the bucket and your cord. When you reach the end of the path from this place, look up in the air." The girl did so, and a beautiful star fell on her brow.

She went home. Her mother ran to meet her and to scold her for being away so long. When she saw the star on her brow, which shone so that it was beautiful to see, she asked, "Where have you been? Who put that star on your forehead?"

The girl answered, "I did not know it was there." Her mother tried to wash it away, but instead of disappearing, it shone more beautifully than ever.

When the girl told what had happened to her, the other sister wanted to go down the well, too. The next day she did the same as her sister. She let the bucket fall, climbed down, and knocked at the saint's door. "Have you found a cord and bucket?"

"No, my child."

She knocked at the next door. "Have you found a cord and bucket?" The devil answered, "No, I have not found them, but come here, my child, come here." But when she heard that he had not found her bucket, the girl said, "No, I will go on."

She knocked at the Madonna's door. "Have you found a cord and bucket?" The Madonna said that she had. "I am going away. You will give my son his broth, and then you will sweep. When I return, I will give you your bucket."

Instead of giving the broth to the child, the bad girl ate it herself. "Oh!" she said, "How good it was!" She swept and found a great deal of dirt. "Oh, poor me! My sister found so many pretty things!"

When the Madonna returned, she asked, "Have you done what I told you?"

"Yes."

"Do you want a brass or a silver thimble?"

"Oh! I want the silver one!" The Madonna gave her the brass one.

"Do you want the calico dress or the silk one?"

"Give me the silk dress."

The Madonna gave her the calico dress. "Here is your bucket and cord. When you are out of here, look up into the air." When the girl was out, she looked up into the air, and there fell on her forehead a lump of dirt that soiled her whole face. She went home in a rage to weep and scold her sister because her sister had the star, while she had dirt on her face. Her mother tried to wash it, but the dirt did not go away.

Then the mother said, "I understand; the Madonna has done this to show me that I loved the bad girl and neglected the good one."

 What one hears is doubtful; what one sees is certain.

Story Notes:

As Catholicism plays an important role in Italian culture, it is not surprising that AT 480 includes a religious figure. The popular motif of choosing an object that reveals the character's humility or greed occurs in this story in the choice of dresses and thimbles. The opening action is similar to that of Mother Holle; in that tale the girl loses her spindle down the well.

> **Motifs:**
> Q2.1.1Da - kind and unkind girls following the river subtype; The Italian Group; The Little Bucket.
> N777.2 - in pursuit of lost bucket
> F725.9 - other world at bottom of well
> G204 - girl in service of witch
> L210 - modest choice
> F545.2.1. - star on forehead as reward
> J2400 - foolish imitation
> Q475.2 - shower of pitch as punishment

29. Blindman's Bluff

RUSSIA

A widowed peasant married a widow, and each had a daughter. Thus, they each had a stepchild. One day the mother said to her husband, "Your daughter Luba is always singing and humming while she spins the flax. If she were by herself, she would not do that, and she would spin more efficiently. Take her to the mud hut in the forest. Let her spend the night there."

Made of clods of earth, the mud hut was used by woodsmen as a place to rest. It was no place for someone to be alone at night. But the girl's father did not know what else to do, so he left her in the hut and said, "Light a fire and keep it burning. Cook yourself some kasha, spin, and always keep the hut locked."

Night came, and the girl cooked her kasha. Suddenly a little mouse ran out and said, "Maiden, give me a spoonful of kasha."

"Oh, little mouse, I was so lonely. I am glad to have your company. You can have more than one spoonful of kasha. Eat as much as you like."

The mouse ate and left, and everything was quiet. Then, at midnight, there was a pounding on the door, it opened, and a bear came into the hut. "Hello," said the bear. "Put out the fire. We are going to play Blindman's Bluff."

Now this was a game often played by Luba and her friends. A child would take a little bell, ring it, and run around trying not to let the person with the blindfold tag her. But whoever had played with a bear? Luba was terrified. Just then the mouse whispered in her ear, "Don't be afraid. Say to him, 'All right.' When he is blindfolded, give me the bell."

Luba said, "All right, bear." Then she put out the fire, gave the bell to the little mouse, and crawled under the stove to hide. The bear could not catch that little mouse. He began to roar and hurl sticks. Finally, tired, he said, "You have won. I will leave a prize for you by the door."

The next morning, the old man's wife said, "Go, old man, and see how well your daughter is doing with her spinning." She was sure the girl would not have survived.

The dog began to bark. "*Bow wow wow*. Your

daughter is coming with a basket of treasure."

"You are lying, dog!" the wife said. But the father and daughter came back carrying a basket filled with honey and berries. "Well! Tonight you will take my daughter to that mud hut in the forest," she said to her husband.

That night the father took his wife's daughter, Natasha, to the mud hut and gave her the same advice. "Here is what you need to make a fire and cook your kasha. Do not let the fire go out. Stay inside and spin. Keep the door locked."

When the girl cooked her gruel, a mouse came out. "Please give me a spoonful of kasha."

"Oh, go away," the girl cried out, and she threw a stick at the mouse.

At midnight, the bear broke into the hut. "Little girl? Let's play Blindman's Bluff." Natasha was so frightened that her teeth rattled. "So, there you are," said the bear. "Here, take this bell and run around. I will try to catch you." Natasha's hand was shaking, and so the bell kept ringing and ringing.

In the morning, the wife sent the old man to the woods. "Bring back my daughter and some good food for us to eat."

The dog barked. "*Bow wow wow wow*. Bones in the basket."

The old woman said, "You are lying, dog!" But her husband came home, sadly holding a basket of bones. The old woman began to scream and cry, and she died that night. But the father and Luba lived out their days in peace. And when Luba married, the father's happiness was complete.

 Reputation is what you are in the light.
Character is what you are in the dark.

U.S. folk wisdom

Story Notes:

According to Iona and Peter Opie in *Children's Games in Street and Playground* (Oxford University Press, 1969 and 1984) pp.117-120, Blind Man's Bluff has been reported as being played in Italy, Germany, Austria, France, Finland, Russia, China, Korea, Japan, India, and Ethiopa. The violent part of the game as it is played in this story is not unprecedented. In classical times, one boy's eyes were covered with a bandage and he shouted out, "I shall chase the brazen fly." The others retorted, "You may chase him but you won't catch him," and they hit him with papyrus husk whips until one of them was caught by the blindfolded player. In the fourteenth century the face of the person who was "it" was covered with a hood and the other players hit him until one of them was caught. The popular children's game, "Pin the Tail on the Donkey" may be a derivative of this game. It is also interesting to note that several variants of this story have a donkey's tail appearing on the forehead of the bad child.

This story is summarized from the following variants: Janet Higgonnet Schnopper, "Daughter and Step Daughter," in *Tales from atop a Russian Stove* (Chicago: Albert Whitman and Co., 1973), 109–117; "Daughter and Step Daughter," in *Russian Fairy Tales* (New York: Pantheon, 1973) 278–279; "Baba Yaga," in *Russian Fairy Tales* (New York: Pantheon, 1973), 194-195. This story, like the other Russian variant, *King Frost*, page 23, has the mother make her husband expose his daughter to abandonment and danger.

Motifs:

Q2.1.3B - Kind and unkind girls; Ogre Kept at Bay subtype; The Blindman's Bluff.

S322 - children abandoned (driven forth, exposed) by hostile relative

Q42.1.1 - child divides last loaf with fairy (witch, etc.)

B210 - speaking animals

B216 - knowledge of animal language. Person understands them.

H1539.1 - bear demands maiden play Blindman's Buff

B431.2 - helpful mouse

B211.7 - dog announces return

Q45 - hospitality rewarded [food in basket]

Q292 - inhospitality punished

Q411 - death

30. Juanita, Marianeta, the Cat, and the Bear

SAN JUAN PUEBLO, AMERICAN INDIAN

h-way-way-ham-by-yoh. An Indian man and woman had two daughters, Juanita and Marianeta. Juanita was older than Marianeta, so whenever their father and mother went to a fiesta (a kind of picnic and dance,) they always took Juanita and left Marianeta at home with the cat.

One day the father and mother and Juanita went to a fiesta to stay all day and all night. That afternoon, when Marianeta was cutting up meat to make a stew for her supper, the cat sat down beside her and begged for some of the meat. Marinita gave her some; then she gave her some water and stroked her fur.

That evening when it began to grow dark, Marianeta was afraid, for there was no one in the house with her, but the cat said, "Don't be afraid. You fasten the door and the windows tight, and I will take care of you."

So Marianeta locked the door and fastened the windows. That night a bear came to the door and knocked. The cat peeped out through a crack to see who was knocking. He saw the bear, for cats can see at night, and he called out, "I am sorry we cannot open the door for you, Bear-man, we are busy making a fire."

The bear waited a while and then knocked again. But the cat said, "We are making bread now, so we cannot open the door."

The bear waited and knocked a third time. "Open the door. I have presents for you."

This time the cat called, "I am sorry, but we are baking the bread and we cannot open the door."

The bear grew tired of waiting. He tried to break the door down, but it was too strong, so he started away. Just then the cat opened the door and jumped out upon the bear's back. It startled the bear, and he dropped a bundle of presents. The bundle fell open, and out fell the most beautiful jewelry and dresses and fine things that Marianeta had ever seen.

The bear was so frightened that he ran away, and Marianeta went out and gathered up all of the beautiful things. She dressed the cat up in a pretty little dress and some beaded shoes that just fit her. Then she dressed herself in a new dress and put on the jewels.

When the father, mother, and Juanita came home next morning, the cat ran out to meet them. They were surprised to see her dress and shoes and wondered what had happened. She told them, but they could not understand her. She told them again, and they still did not understand, so they went into the house in a hurry to see what the cat meant. They were so pleased to see Marianeta looking so fine that they hugged her up tight.

"Where did you get these lovely things?"

Marianeta told them all about the bear. The next time there was a fiesta, Juanita decided to stay home and let Marianeta go with their father and mother. She wanted the bear to bring her some pretty things.

That afternoon, when Juanita was cutting up meat for stew, the cat sat beside her and begged for some of the meat, but Juanita would not give her any. Instead she struck at the cat with her knife and treated her mean. The cat climbed up on the window and went to sleep. When it grew dark, Juanita began to feel afraid at being all alone. The cat pretended to still be asleep. She did not say anything to Juanita about the door and windows, and Juanita did not think to fasten them. That night, when the bear came to knock on the door, he found the door unlocked, so he walked right into the house. Juanita thought he had come to bring her some fine clothes, so she said, "Good evening, Bear-man, won't you have a seat?" and the bear sat down beside her.

"What makes your feet so big, Bear-man?"

"To walk the faster, little one."

"Well, what makes your nose so long?"

"To scent the keener, little girl."

"And what makes your ears so big?"

"To hear the better, my dear."

"What makes your eyes so bright?"

"To see the further."

"What makes your teeth so long?"

"To eat you up."

And the bear ran away with Juanita, planning to eat her up.

But when Marianeta came home and the cat saw how she grieved for her sister, she ran to the bear's den, jumped on the back of the bear's head, scratched out his eyes, and brought Juanita back home again.

 You'll never plough a field by turning it over in your mind.

Irish proverb

Story Notes:

This story comes from a book called *Taytay's Tales,* which means "Grandfather's Stories." Note the similarity to the story of "Little Red Riding Hood." The Indian storyteller who told this tale to the anthropologist collecting stories for this book said that this tale was "already very old when my grandfather heard it."

Pueblo is the Spanish word for "people." When the Spaniards saw the unusual two- and three-story- high, flat-topped buildings that the Indians in the Southwest lived in, they called them "people houses."

This story is from the Tewas, who always begin their tales, "Oh-way-way-ham-by-yoh," (Once upon a time, long ago).

> **Motifs:**
> Q42.1.1 - child divides last loaf with fairy, witch, etc.
> Q40 - kindness rewarded
> B210 - speaking animals
> B216 - knowledge of animal language
> B422 - helpful cat
> Q280 - unkindness punished
> R157.1 - heroine rescues sister

31. The Blind Beggar

ICELAND

It happened on a certain farm that some children had gone out to play beside a knoll: one little girl and two boys older than her. They saw a hole in the knoll, and then this girl who was the youngest among them took it into her head to stick her hand right inside the hole and to say as a joke, as children often do:

"The old man's blind, the old man's blind,

Lay a little something in the old man's hand!"

Then a large gilded button for her apron was laid in the child's hand.

As soon as the other children saw this, they were jealous. The eldest said he would go next, and he stuck his hand right in, saying the same as the youngest had said, expecting that this would get him a surprise at least as fine as she had gotten. But it did not work out like that, for this boy received nothing at all; and, what's more, when he took his hand out of the hole, it had withered, and it remained that way all his life.

 Who seeks what he should not, finds what he would not.

German proverb

Story Notes:

In this story, the first child, innocently pretending she is playing a game, is surprisingly rewarded. The other children should have figured out that this was an elf abode and remembered that Icelandic elves are quick to punish greed and jealousy and to resent ill-mannered intrusions on their privacy.

This story is told as a legend, whereas the other stories in this book are classified as folk tales. A legend is a story that purports to be true — someone, somewhere, at some time believed it. The plot hinges on credibility, and legends are told about real people and are often identified with a specific site. Folk tales include fantasy and may be symbolic, with personal attributes symbolically represented in actions and objects.

Blind Beggar is a children's game played in Iceland. It is similar to a game played in England and the United States in which one person says, "Open your mouth and close your eyes, and I will give you a nice surprise." Something — usually a treat — is then placed on the tongue of the child who has his or her eyes closed. When I was a young, however, I deviated from the standard treat and put cayenne on my sister's tongue. She always mentions that incident when she is telling someone how hard it was to be an older sister.

Motifs:
    F340 - gifts from fairies [elves]
    Q301 - jealousy punished

32 The Servant at the Fairies

BASQUE, SPAIN

Once upon a time there was a woman who had three daughters. One day the youngest said to her mother that she had decided to go out and find work. She went from town to town, until it happened that she came to a village of laminaks (fairies) and a fairy asked her, "Where are you going, my child?"

She answered, "Do you know a place for a servant?"

"Yes. If you will come to my house, I will hire you."

The girl went there, and the fairy said, "We are fairies. I must go from home, but your work is in the kitchen. Smash the pitcher, break all the plates, pound the children, make them fix their own breakfast, make their faces dirty, and rumple their hair."

The fairy left, and a little dog came to the girl and said, "*Tchau, tchau, tchow;* I too, I want something."

"Be off from here, silly little dog; I will give you a kick."

But the dog did not go away; and at last the girl gave him something to eat, a little, not much.

"And now," says he, "I will tell you what the mistress has told you to do. She told you to sweep the kitchen, to fill the pitcher, and to wash all the plates, to feed the children and wash their faces and brush their hair. When that is all well done she will give you the choice of a sack of charcoal or a bag of gold; and the choice of a beautiful star on your forehead or a donkey's tail hanging from it. You must answer, "A sack of charcoal and a donkey's tail.""

The fairy returned. The new servant had done all the work, and the fairy was very well satisfied with her. So she said, "Choose which you would like, a sack of charcoal or a bag of gold."

"A sack of charcoal is the same to me."

"A star for your forehead, or a donkey's tail?"

"A donkey's tail would be the same to me."

Then the girl was given a bag of gold and a beautiful star on her forehead. She went home, and she was so pretty with this star and carrying a bag of gold on her shoulders that the whole family was astonished.

The next day the eldest daughter said, "Mother, I will go and be a servant too."

Her mother did not want her to go. "No, my child, you shall not do so."

But as the girl would not leave her mother in peace, the mother finally assented. The girl went off and finally came to the city of the fairies, where she met the same fairy as her sister had. The fairy asked, "Where are you going, my girl?"

"To be a servant."

"Come to my house."

And she took the girl as servant. She told her, like the first one, "You will dig up the kitchen, break the plates, smash the pitcher, make the children fix their own breakfast, dirty their faces, and rumple their hair."

There was some of the breakfast left over, and the little dog came in and said "*Tchow! tchow! tchow!* I too, I should like something." And he followed her everywhere, but she gave him nothing and drove him off with kicks.

When the fairy came home, she found the kitchen all dug up, the pitcher and all the plates broken, and the children hungry and dirty. Then she asked the servant, "What do you ask for wages? A bag of gold or a sack of charcoal? A star on your forehead or a donkey's tail?"

The girl chose the bag of gold and the star on her forehead but instead received a sack of charcoal and a donkey's tail for her forehead. She went home crying and told her mother that she was very sorry.

Now the second daughter, the middle sister, asked permission to go. "No! No!" said the mother, and made her stay at home.

❦ *We are the authors of our own disasters.* ❦

Latin proverb

Footnote:

Basque Laminak always say exactly the contrary to what they mean for you to do.

Story Notes:

The interchanging of a powerful woman figure and magical fairies as the donor (employer) in Tale Type 480 is partially explained by noting that "Diamonds and Toads (page 105), one of the best known Tale Type 480 variants, was originally published as "The Fairy."

Motifs:

Q2 - kind and unkind girls

G204 - girl in service of witch{fairy}

F200 - fairies

F210 - fairyland

H580.1. - girl given enigmatic commands, must do the opposite

B210 - speaking animals

B216 - knowledge of animal language. Person understands them.

B421 - helpful dog

B5662.3 - helper advises which reward to choose

L210 - modest choice

Q3 - modest request rewarded, immodest punished

Q111 - riches as reward

F545.2.1 - reward: star on forehead

J2400 - foolish imitation

Q580 - punishment fitted to crime

33. The Legend of Knockgrafton

IRELAND

here was once a poor man who lived in the fertile glen of Aherlow, at the foot of the gloomy Galtee Mountains, who had a great hump on his back. His head was pressed down with so much weight that he walked all hunched over. People avoided him, although he was a very nice man, and rather shy. He made his living with his skillful hands, plaiting straw and rushes into hats and baskets.

No one knew his real name, but everyone called him Lusmore because he always wore a sprig of the fairy cap, or Lusmore (foxglove), in his straw hat.

One evening Lusmore was returning from the pretty town of Cahir, walking home toward Cappagh. He always walked slowly, on account of the hump on his back, and so it was quite dark when he came to the old moat of Knockgrafton, which stood on the right-hand side of the road. Tired and weary was he, and noways comfortable in his own mind at thinking how much further he had to travel and that he should be walking all night. So he sat down under the moat to rest himself and began looking mournfully up at the full moon in the night sky.

As he sat there, there rose a wild strain of unearthly melody. He thought he had never heard such ravishing music before. It was like the sound of many voices, each mingling and blending with the other so strangely that they seemed to be one, though all singing different strains, and the words of the song were these: "Monday, Tuesday, Monday, Tuesday, Monday Tuesday." Then there was a brief pause and it began again. "Monday, Tuesday, Monday, Tuesday, Monday, Tuesday."

Lusmore listened attentively, scarcely drawing his breath. But after a while, this music, which had charmed him so much at first, sounded repetitive. He began to get tired of hearing the same words and melody sung over and over without any change. So, availing himself of the pause after the third "Monday, Tuesday," he took up the tune and raised it, adding "'Wednesday," and then he went on singing with the voices coming from the moat, and on the third round they all sang "Wednesday" with him.

This song was a fairy melody, and when the fairies within Knockgrafton heard this addition to the tune, they were so delighted that, with instant resolve, it was determined to bring the mortal among them. They liked the way he added his voice to theirs, they were happy to have some new words to sing, and he had a fine singing voice as well.

Lusmore was conveyed into their company with the eddying speed of a whirlwind. Glorious to behold was the sight that burst upon him as he came down through the moat, twirling round and round, with the lightness of a straw. He was in a beautiful place with beautiful fairies all about. The greatest honor was then paid him. Then they came to him and said,

"Lusmore! Lusmore!

Doubt not, nor deplore

For the hump which you bore

On your back is no more;

Look down on the floor

And view it, Lusmore!"

When these words were said, Lusmore felt himself so light that he felt like he could have jumped right over that full moon. Then he fell asleep.

When he awoke, it was broad daylight, with the sun shining brightly and the birds sweetly singing. He was lying just at the foot of the moat of Knockgrafton. Cows and sheep were grazing peacefully about him. He reached behind to feel his hump, but it wasn't there! And he found himself wearing a full suit of new clothes, which he concluded that the fairies had made for him.

Toward Cappagh he went, stepping as lightly and springing at every step as if he had been all his life a dancing master. Of course it was not long before the story of Lusmore's hump got about, and a great wonder was made of it. Through the country for miles round, it was the talk of everyone, high and low.

One morning as Lusmore was sitting contented enough at his cabin door, up came an old woman and asked if he could direct her to Cappagh.

"I need give you no directions, my good woman," said Lusmore, "for this is Cappagh; and whom may you want here?"

"I have come," said the woman, "from the county of Waterford looking after one Lusmore, who, I have heard tell, had his hump taken off by the fairies; for there is a son of mine who has got a hump on him that will be his death."

Lusmore, who was ever good-natured, told the woman all the particulars, how he had raised the tune for the fairies at Knockgrafton on the night of a full moon, how his lump had been removed from his shoulders, and how he had gotten a new suit of clothes into the bargain.

The woman thanked him very much and went away quite happy. She went back and told her son, who had been peevish and cunning from his birth, that he should do exactly what Lusmore had done. The next full moon she put him in a cart and brought him all the way to Knockgrafton and left him by the moat.

Jack Madden, for that was the man's name, had not been sitting there long when he heard the tune. "Monday, Tuesday, Monday, Tuesday, Monday, Tuesday, Wednesday." So he shouted out, "Thursday and Friday! Thursday and Friday!" thinking if one day was good, two days would be even better.

No sooner had the words passed his lips than he was whisked into the moat with fairies crowded around him saying, "You spoiled our tune!"

"Jack Madden! Jack Madden!
Your words came so bad in
The tune we felt glad in
The castle you're had in
That your life we may sadden:
Here's two humps for Jack Madden."

And twenty of the strongest fairies brought Lusmore's hump and put it on poor Jack's back where it became fixed as firmly as if it were nailed with twelve-penny nails by the best carpenter that ever drove one.

The next morning Jack's mother found him. And whether it was the second hump or the long journey, he died soon after, saying he would curse anyone who would want to listen to fairy tunes.

 More have repented speech than silence.

English proverb

Story Notes:

In these AT 480 tales, the hero or heroine must successfully pass a test or other preconditions to receive the reward. In this story, not only does Lusmore sing pleasantly, he also wears the flower known as fairy cap, or lusmore, in *his* cap, a flower which resembles a tiny fairy cap.

In many Irish tales, fairy music, "Ceol Sidhe," is heard in the vicinity of fairy dwellings.

While this story has the removal and addition of a hunchback as the reward and punishment, AT 480 collected from Japanese oral tradition, has the men with a wen, or lump, on the face. Roberts lists twenty-three Japanese variants of "How an Old Man Loses His

Wen" in *The Kind and Unkind*. In one well-known Japanese variation, a man is asked to leave the wen on his face as a guarantee that he will return to dance with the Oni (monsters) again. The second man dances poorly and is unmannerly. The Onis (who cannot tell one human from another) say, "You do not need to come back again. Here is your wen back," so he leaves with two wens on his face.

Motifs:

Q.1 - kind and unkind

F210 - fairyland

F320 - fairies carry people away to fairyland

330 - grateful fairies

Q41 - politeness [waited for pause in tune]

Q41 - politeness rewarded

F331.3 - mortal wins fairies' gratitude by joining in their song

F370 - visit to fairyland

F344.1 - fairies remove hunchback's hump (or replace it)

D1960 - magic sleep

F340 - gift from fairies - new suit of clothes

F344.1.3. - fairies remove hunchback's hump.

J2400 - foolish imitation

Q556 - cursed [by fairies]

W187 - insolence

Q551.8 - deformity as punishment

III

SUMMARIES OF ADDITIONAL TEXTS

34. Africa

A father with two daughters learns that a chief on the other side of the river is looking for a wife. The older daughter insists on going by herself, even though it is unheard of for a bride to go to her wedding without friends and family. She meets a mouse, who politely offers her directions. She is rude to the mouse, who shrieks, "Bad luck to you." This is repeated with a frog and a little boy driving goats. She meets an old woman, who tells her what to do when she sees laughing trees, milk, and a man carrying his head under his arm. The girl is rude to the old woman and disobeys her instructions. Entering the village, she meets the chief's sister, and she is rude to her as well. She is asked to fix a meal, which she does badly. The chief appears as a snake with five heads and eats her. The second daughter decides to go to this village and sets out with musicians and drummers. She is courteous to the mouse, the frog, the little boy with the goats, the old woman, and the chief's sister. She prepares a delicious meal. When she marries the snake chief, his snakeskin disappears, and he becomes a handsome man.

"The Snake Chief," in *African Myths and Legends,* retold by Kathleen Arnott (New York: Henry Z. Walck, 1968), pp.186–194.

> **Motifs:**
> Q2.1.2Ea - kind and unkind girls encounters en route subtype: African and Afro-American tradition.
> F721 - subterranean world
> F127 - journey to animal kingdom
> C50 - offending gods
> C94 - tabu: rudeness to sacred person/thing
> Q411 - death
> D731 - disenchantment by obedience and kindness

35. Austria

A rich brother and a poor brother live across the street from each other. Saint Nicholas, covered with dust so he looks like a common beggar, is refused lodging by the rich brother. The poor brother welcomes him, and he and his wife offer all they have, which is only brown bread and water from the town fountain. Nicholas makes food and drink appear, and the bowl and pitcher remain filled to the brim, no matter how much they eat or drink. The rich brother cons his brother out of the bowl and pitcher but can't make them stop, and food and drink fill his house. He has to pay the poor brother to take them back. Saint Christopher decides to roam, and Saint Nicholas suggests he visit the hospitable poor man and his wife. He is refused hospitality at the rich brother's house but receives a warm welcome at the poor brother's house. The wife makes him a new shirt while he sleeps, and the husband offers the saint his money. The saint tells them, "Whatever you begin doing this morning, you shall continue doing till sunset." They can't decide what to do, so the man starts to put the money away and the woman to fold linen. By sunset the home is filled with linens and silver. The rich brother finds out about this and asks his brother to promise to send any additional saints that come by over to his house. A year and a day later, both saints come together for a visit. The kind couple tell them that their brother has asked that they come there. This time the rich couple feed their guests and give them new shirts. They are told, "Whatever you begin doing this morning, you shall continue doing till sunset." They can't decide what to do, so the wife goes to fill the pig troughs and finds she cannot stop. Her husband is so angry he picks up a stick to beat her and cannot stop till sunset. The neighbors hear the noise, come, and laugh. The story ends, "For even the blessed saints cannot give wisdom to those who will have none of it, and that is the truth."

"How the Good Gifts Were Used by Two," in Howard Pyle, *The Wonder Clock* (New York: Harper and Row, 1887, ©1915), pp. 123-133.

Motifs:
Q1.1 - Gods (saints) in disguise hospitality rewarded; inhospitality punished
J2073.1.1 -wise and foolish wishes
Q42 - sharing food
Q45 - hospitality rewarded
D1472.2 - magic food supplier
D1652.1 - inexhaustible food
J2415 - foolish imitation of lucky man
D1651.3 - magic cooking pot obeys only master
Q292.1 - inhospitality to saint punished

36. Brittany

A rich widower with a sweet daughter marries an ugly and envious widow with a daughter of the same nature. The good daughter is sent to empty the garbage into the sea and mistakenly drops the bucket into the water. A sea monster and three mermaids appear, and the mermaids ask the girl to comb their hair. They give her a golden dress, fill her bucket with pearls, and place a star on her forehead. The cruel girl attempts the same and ends with a donkey tail on her forehead.

"The Three Mermaids," in Ruth Manning-Sanders, *A Choice of Magic*, ill. Robin Jacques (New York: E. P. Dutton & Co., 1971), pp.280–290.

Motifs:
B81 - mermaid
H1192 - combing hair
F545.2.1 - star on forehead as reward

37. Chile

A woodcutter finds four dwarfs and teaches them a song, "Monday and Tuesday, Wednesday three, with Thursday, Friday, Saturday, six." The dwarfs give the woodcutter four wishes. He wishes for food, clothing, money and a home. His rich, selfish brother finds the dwarfs, adds "and Sunday seven" to the song. They give him four wishes. His wife foolishly wishes for a beard on her baby. The next wish is to take it off. Her husband is so angry he wishes the beard stuck to her, and so the last wish is to take it off. "This is what happens to the envious." (Note the similarity of this tale to the well-known "The Three Wishes" " in *More English Fairy Tales*, by Joseph Jacobs (New York: G.P. Putnam's Sons, 1894) pp. 107-109.) In this story, the woodcutter is granted three wishes by a fairy and in hunger wishes for a sausage. His wife, in anger at his wasting the wish, wishes it were stuck to his nose. Their third wish, therefore, is to take it off. At least they had a fine sausage for dinner!

"The Four Little Dwarfs," in Yolanda Pino-Saavedra, ed., *Folktales of Chile*, trans. Rockwell Gray (University of Chicago Press, 1970), pp. 85–89.

Motifs:
F331.3 - mortal wins fairies gratitude by joining in their song
F341 - fairies grant wishes

38. China

A man tends a bird and is rewarded with a pumpkin seed. He grows a pumpkin, which is found to be filled with gold and silver. A cruel child deliberately harms a swallow and tends it, and he, too, receives a pumpkin seed. But out of his pumpkin steps an old man. Runners from the pumpkin shoot up to the sky, and the man takes the boy up this ladder to the Palace of Boundless Cold on the moon. To return home, he has to cut down a tree that is made of gold with branches covered with stones and agates. With each blow of his axe, however, a rooster bites him. He remains there to this day. If you look up at the moon, you can see the tree, the boy, and the Palace of Boundless Cold.

"The Man Who Cuts Down the Cinnamon Tree," in *Chinese Fairy Tales and Folktales*, collected and trans. by Wolfram Eberhard (New York: E. P. Dutton & Co., 1938), pp. 200–202.

> **Motifs:**
> Q42 - generosity rewarded
> A751.1.8 - punishment for huting bird - climbs to moon and remains there
> J2415.13 - seed as reward for helping wounded bird

39. England

Two girls live with their mother and father. One girl wanted to go into service and could not find a position in town, so she went on into the country. She met an oven, and the bread said, "Little girl, little girl, take us out. We have been baking seven years, and no one has come to take us out." She did this. Then she met a cow, who said, "Little girl, little girl, milk me, milk me! Seven years have I been waiting, and no one has come to milk me." She does this. As she was thirsty, she drank some, and she left the rest in the pails by the cow. She meets an and helps an apple tree, and then goes on till she came to a house where a witch lived who took girls into her house as servants and who told her that she would try her and give her good wages. The witch told the girl, "You must never look up the chimney, or something bad will befall you."

The girl forgot what the witch had said, and she looked up the chimney. When she did this, a great bag of money fell down in her lap. She took the money and ran off.

When she had gone some way, she heard the witch coming after her. So she ran to the apple tree and cried:

"Apple tree, apple tree, hide me,
So the old witch can't find me.

If she does, she'll pick my bones.

And bury me under the marble stones."

So the apple tree hid her. When the witch came up, she said,

"Tree of mine, tree of mine,

Have you seen a girl

With a willy-willy way and a long-tailed bag

Who stole my money, all I had?"

And the apple tree said, "No, mother, not for seven years."

This was repeated with the cow and the oven. Then the baker told the witch to look in the oven, and he shut the door. Later, she was able to get out, but the girl had already reached her home with her money bags.

The other sister then thought she would go and do the same. But she refused to help the bread, the cow, or the tree. She, too, looked up the chimney, and down fell a bag of money. She ran off. However, the tree told the witch which way she had gone so the old witch caught her. She took all the money away, beat her, and sent her home just as she was.

"The Old Witch," in *More English Fairy Tales*, collected by Joseph Jacobs (New York: Dover, 1967, originally 1898) pp. 94-97, notes p. 230.

> **Motifs:**
> See "The Old Hag's Long Leather Bag," page 78
>   "The Two Stepsisters," page 95
>   "Mother Holle," page 34

40. Eskimo

Two rich couples each have a daughter. They both live near a poor old woman living with her grandson. While one of the girls is cruel to the boy, the other brings food so he will not starve. One day the grandmother magically creates a whale, which they cut up and store for food. The boy asks his grandmother to go to the house of the girl who brought food to see if she will marry him. The grandmother goes to the wrong house, however, and the people there are cruel to her. Then she goes to the right house. When the second girl goes to his house, she finds that the grandmother has made new clothes for her and has gifts for her parents. The rich man tries to sell his daughter to the boy, but the boy does not want her. Later that family disappears, and it is presumed they have starved.

"The Two Rich Girls," in Edwin S. Hall, Jr., *The Eskimo Storyteller* (Knoxville: The University of Tennessee Press, 1975), pp. 95–97.

41. Haiti

A serving girl ordered to find it a teaspoon lost in the river meets an old woman, who asks the girl to wash her back. Her hands, cut from the old woman's back, are healed when the old woman spits on them. The old woman gives her banana pudding. The next day, she is able to make a casserole with a bone, a grain of rice, and one bean. Although told not to give the cat any milk, the girl disobeys. When she leaves, the woman tells her that she will see eggs, and the larger ones will say, "Take me," but she should take the smaller ones. The girl does, and out of the eggs come silverware. The woman she works for has a daughter who decides to do the same, but she insults the old woman and beats the cat. She opens the largest egg and out come lizards and demons. (Note the power of spittle in this story, as in "Spiola," page 33. Note, also, the similarity of choosing eggs with "The Talking Eggs," page 102, and "The Brothers and the Eggs," page 68.)

"Mother of the Waters," Diane Wolkstein, in *The Magic Orange Tree* (Schocken, 1980, 1996), pp. 153-156.

Motifs:
Q2.1.2H - Kind and unkind girls, encounters en route subtype; Servant girl sent to find teaspoon
D1652.1 - Inexhaustible food
D2105 - provisions magically furnished
G219.9 - witch's back covered with nails and broken glass
L215 - main actor told to take objects that say "Don't take me"
L220 - modest request best
D1450 - magic object furnishes treasure [egg]
J2400 - foolish imitation

42 Iran

An evil sister tricks an enchantress and receives a magical pearl necklace intended for her sister. With her new powers, she turns her sister into a cat. She is to be queen, but when the crown is placed on her head at the coronation, the necklace tightens around her throat. When she confesses and turns her sister back into a girl, the necklace disappears. She is punished by having to take care of hundreds of cats. When she vows to mend her wicked ways, she is relieved of this duty, and she is faithful to her word.

"Moon Pearls," in Jean Russell Larson, *Palace in Bagdad*, ill. Matianne Yamaguchi (New York: Charles Scribner & Sons, 1966).

43. Italy

A stepdaughter loses her basket, which is swept off by the stream. She follows the river, searching for it, and meets an old woman, who says she has the basket and asks what is biting her back. The girl sees vermin but answers, "Pearls and diamonds," so as not to embarrass the old woman. There is a series of choices, questions, and chores. The girl always chooses the humbler gift, and she returns with riches and a star on her brow. Her envious stepsister follows the same route but returns with a donkey tail on her forehead. Through a mix-up, the mother scalds and kills her own daughter.

"Water in the Basket," in *Italian Folktales*, selected and retold by Italo Calvino, trans. George Martin, (New York: Harcourt Brace Jovanovich, 1980), pp. 353–355.

Motifs:
F545.21 - star on forehead as reward
Q41.2 - reward for cleansing loathsome person
L210 - choosing humber gift

44. Italy

The ill-treated stepdaughter is sent to pick chicory. She picks, instead, a large cauliflower, and seeing a hole in the ground where she pulled it up, she goes down. She finds a house full of cats and helps them with their chores. The mama cat serves her macaroni, meat, and roast chicken, while the other cats are served only beans. She shares her food with the cats. She chooses the humblest gifts they offer her, but they give her the best and put a star on her brow and rings on her fingers. Now the stepmother sends her daughter, and she is disagreeable to the cats. The mama cat serves the girl barley cake soaked in vinegar, but the girl steals food from the cats' plates. She is sent home with worms on her fingers and a blood sausage on her face, which she has to nibble constantly to keep it from growing.

"The Tale of the Cats/Colony of Cats," in *Italian Folktales*, selected and retold by Italo Calvino, Tale 129 (New York: Harcourt Brace Jovanovich, 1980), pp. 446–448, story notes on p. 741.

Motifs:
D1652.1 - inexhaustible food
See "House of Cats," page 110

45. Japan

An old woman cares for a sparrow with a broken leg, and the bird, when healed, returns with a seed. This grows into an enormous vine filled with gourds, which she shares with the village. A few gourds she saves to dry, and when she opens them, they are filled with rice. No matter how much rice she takes from them, the gourds remain a perpetual source of rice.

An envious neighbor throws stones at three sparrows and breaks their legs. Then she tends these birds. When they are healed, they fly off and bring her back some seeds, which she plants. However, the gourds that grow on her vine are bitter. She saves a few gourds to dry, but when she opens them, they are filled with lizards, horseflies, snakes, wasps, and centipedes.

"The Sparrow's Gifts," in *Japanese Tales* selected and trans. by Royal Tyler (New York: Pantheon Books, 1987) pp. 5-8.

> **Motifs:**
> D1652.1 - inexhaustible food
> See "The Sparrow's Gift," page 38

46. Japan

A kind woodcutter who never cut off branches from living trees found a tree with the sap seeping out from where someone had torn off branches. When he ripped his clothes to wrap around these places gold and silver fell from the tree. Another woodcutter, the very one who had torn off the three branches, found out about the gold and silver and went to the tree. The tree showered him with sticky-sticky sap. It took three days for the sap to become soft enough for him to drag himself home. "And after that, he never broke another branch off a living tree."

"The Sticky-Sticky Pine," in Florence Sakade, ed., *Peach Boy and Other Japanese Children's Favorite Stories*, ill. Yoshisuke Kurosaki (Rutland, Vt: Charles E. Tuttle Co., 1958).

> **Motifs:**
> D2171.1.0.1 - Woodcutter mends three broken branches of pine.
> Q2 - kind and unkind
> F811 - extraordinay tree
> F962 - extraordinary shower [gold]
> D2100 - magic wealth
> J2415 - foolish imitation of lucky man
> Q475.2 - pitch shower as punishment
> Q580 - punishment fitted to crime (pitch sticks 3 days; 3 broken branches)

47. Japan

A woodcutter lost a rice ball down a hole. He heard singing about the rice ball, so he dropped another ball into the hole. He heard more singing and a mouse popped up and invited him to visit. He did, and the mice gave him special rice cakes. When it was time to leave, they told him to choose a chest. He chose the smallest, and when he got home, he found that it was filled with gold. A neighbor went down the hole and scared the mice away by saying "*meow*," so that he could take *all* the chests. He could not find his way out, and his wife, seeing something scratching up through the ground, beat it with a stick, only to discover it was her husband's head. "And so it was that the greedy man and his wife lived the rest of their days dreaming of the gold they might have had, while their neighbors enjoyed a long life of ease and comfort."

"The Rolling Rice Ball," by Junicha Yoda, ill. Saburo Watanabe, trans. by Alvin Tresselt (New York: Parents Magazine Press, 1969). This book was translated from *Omusubi Koronin*, originally published by Kasei Sha Publishing Company, Tokyo, Japan.

Motifs:
N777. - dropped ball leads to adventure
N777.0.3 - dumpling [rice ball] rolls down hole.
B221.2 is cited in Thompson as "Kingdom of Rats"
B221.5 - land of mice
Q42 - generosity rewarded
B210 - speaking animals
B216 - knowledge of animal language
L210 - modest choice
Q111 - riches as reward
Q140 - marvelous or magic reward
W151 - greed
J2415 - foolish imitation of lucky man
Q280 - unkindness punished
Q411 - death as punishment

48. Japan

When an old man's dog is killed by a wicked neighbor, he plants a pine tree over the dog's grave and then makes a bowl from the pine wood. Rice magically appears in this bowl. The neighbor asks to borrow the bowl, but instead of rice, it fills with stones, so he burns the bowl. The old man collects the ashes and sprinkles them on bare winter trees growing in his garden. Blossoms magically appear. A prince, delighted with the blossoms, rewards him. The greedy neighbor throws ashes around his tree, which blow into the prince's face, and he is sent to jail.

"Old Man of the Flowers," in *The Dancing Kettle and Other Japanese Folktales* told by Yoshiba Uchida (New York: Harcourt Brace & Co., 1949); also in paperback (Berkeley: Creative Arts Book Co., 1986).

Motifs:
D1652.1 - inexhaustible food

49. Portugal

A schoolmistress who is a widow with a plain daughter wants to marry a man who has a pretty daughter. The school mistress tells the pretty girl to tell her father to marry her, promising the girl porridge made with honey. He doesn't want to marry her, but to please his daughter, he says he will make a pair of iron boots, and when they have rusted to pieces he will marry the schoolmistress. The schoolmistress has the girl wet the boots every day. As a result, they rust, so he marries her. The woman is mean to the pretty girl after the marriage, giving her unreasonable tasks to perform. The girl is helped by a cow and fairies — and receives the gift of gold and pearls falling from her lips when she speaks. They call her "the hearth cat." This story continues as a Cinderella story with beautiful dresses and a lost slipper.

"The Hearth Cat," in *Portuguese Folk-Tales*, collected by Consiglieri Pedroso and trans. by Henriqueta Monteiro (Folk- Lore Society: Kraus Reprint, Nendeln/Lichtenstin, 1967) pp. 75–79.

Motifs:
D1454.2 - treasure falls from mouth

50. Scotland

"There was before now a poor woman, and she had a leash of daughters." The oldest girl decided to go out and seek her fortune. Her mother offered her a choice of taking her blessing or a big bannock and her mother's curse. She chose the bannock. Before long she met the sreath chileanach. (The sreath chileanach is a human sorceress shape-changer, who often appears as a giant female black dog traveling with a flock of pups.) The sreath chileanach asked for some of the bannock, which the girl refused to share.

The girl was hired to watch a dead man throughout the night, but she fell asleep and was struck dead. The same thing happened to the youngest daughter.

The middle daughter took her mother's blessing and shared her food. She did not fall asleep. The man kept sitting up, and when she went to strike him, they were both stuck to the stick. He took her on a run through the woods, and when they returned, she was given gold and silver and a cordial, which, when rubbed on her sisters, brought them back to life. "They returned home; they left me sitting here, and if they were well, 'tis well; and if they were not, let them be."

Note: Usually it is the oldest or youngest girl who is successful. In this story, however, it is the middle child!

"The Girl and the Dead Man," in *Popular Tales of the West Highlands*, vol. 1, orally collected with a trans. by J. F. Campbell (London: Wildwood House, 1963).

> **Motifs:**
> J229.3 - large cake with curse or small cake with mother's blessing
> H1199.1 - heroine must sit up with a corpse
> See "The Corpse Watchers," page 74

IV

ADDITIONAL SUMMARIES
INCLUDED IN THE
STORY NOTES

V

ADDITIONAL CITATIONS

Brazil

(57) "The Golden Gourd," in Francis Carpenter, *South American Wonder Tales* (New York: Follett Publishing Co., 1969).

Burma

(58) "The Happy Ending," in Maung Htin Aung, *Selections from Burmese Folk-tales* (Geoffrey Cumberlege: Oxford University Press, 1951).

Japan

(59) "The Tongue-Cut Sparrow," in *The Japanese Fairy Book*, compiled by Yei Theodora Ozarki (Rutland, Vt.: Charles E. Tuttle Co., 1977) pp. 12–23.

(60) "The Tongue-Cut Sparrow," in *The Dancing Kettle and Other Japanese Folk-Tales*, retold by Yoshiko Uchida, (Creative Arts, 1986, pap.).

(61) "The Sparrow's Gift," in *Japanese Tales*, selected, ed. and trans.by Royall Tyler (New York: Pantheon Books, 1987), pp. 5-8.

Spain

(62) "Tonino and the Fairies," a story by Ralph Steele Boggs and Mary Gould Davis, in *Best Loved Folktales of the World*, ed. By Johanna Cole (N.Y.: Anchor, 1983, pap.). This is a Spanish version of "The Old Man and the Wen," page 133, and "The Legend of Knockgrafton" page 131.

USA

(63) "The Girl Who Gave Breadfruit" retold by Caroline Cutis, in *Hawai`i Island Legends*, Honolulu: Kamehameha Schools Press, 1996. Reprint of Pikoi and Other Legends of the Island of Hawai`i, 1949). pp. 51-55.

Note: Breadfruit grows on trees and is a food staple in Caribbean, South American and other tropical countries. In this story the two girls are together on the journey and when an old woman asks for food one says, "Why help a stranger?" and the other explains that she would want someone to help her grandmother if she was alone and hungry. This story and "The Gift of the Mermaid," page 63, are the only variants in this collection where the kind and unkind protagonists journey together.

(64) "Gallymanders," in *Grandfather Tales*, selected and edited by Richard Chase (Boston, Mass: Houghton Mifflin Company, 1948) pp. 18-28.

VI
PICTURE BOOKS RELATED TO
TALE TYPE 480

China

(65) Demi, *Chen Ping and his Magic Axe* (New York: Dodd, Mead & Co., 1989). A variation of Aesop's fable *The Woodcutter and His Axe.*

(66) Sanfield, Steve, *Just Rewards* (New York: Orchard Books, 1996). A variation of The Tongue-Cut Sparrow.

(67) Demi, *The Empty Pot* (New York: Henry Holt & Co., 1990). This story has a different twist. The little boy who gains the gifts "does his best," while the other children or their parents are dishonest.

Ethiopia

(68) Frank P. Araujo, *The Perfect Orange,* ill. Xiao Jun Li (Windsor, Calif.: Rayve Productions, 1994). A little girl brings the ruler a perfect orange and is rewarded with gifts of gold and jewels. A man, thinks, "If she got all that for an orange, what will the ruler give me for my cattle and lands?" The ruler gives him a perfect orange!

Korea

(69) Older Brother, Younger Brother, retold by Nina Jaffe, ill. Wenhai Ma, (N.Y.: Viking, 1995). The wounded sparrow's gifts of magical gourds ends with the evil brother having a change of heart at the end of the tale.

(70) Hungblu Nolbu: Two Brothers and Their Magic Gourds, by Edward B. Adams, ill. Dong Ho Choi (Seoul International Tourist Publishing Co., 1981). Bilingual.

Poland

(71) *The Rumor of Pauel and Paali*, adapted by Carole Kismaric, ill. Charles Mikolaycak (New York: Harper and Row, 1988).

United States

(72) The Talking Eggs: A Folktale from the American South, retold by Robert D. San Souci, ill. Jerry Pinkney (New York: Dial Books, 1989).

VII
SCRIPTS AND GAMES

Strawberries in The Snow:

Puppet Play Script for Three - Six Puppeteers

Characters:
Mother
Natasha (daughter with strong resemblance to mother)
Luba (daughter)
Fall and Winter (two-headed puppet)
Spring and Summer (two-headed puppet)

Puppeteer one: Mother and Fall/Winter
Puppeteer two: Natasha and Spring/Summer in scene two
Puppeteer three: Luba and Spring/Summer in scene four
You will need:
basket
bright red strawberries
snow (cotton balls or salt crystals)
trees
two boxes (one large and two small)
broom
fire (tiny flashlight hidden under colored paper or colored cardboard in shape
of flames)
bees (a glove with bees on the end of each finger; or ten clear straws stuck in
clay, playdough, or a florist's "frog" with a bee attached to the other end
of each. If you have a broken umbrella, use a metal liner to attach a cloth
or paper bee onto the tip. Hold the other in your hand; slight move-
ments effectively create the effect of a bee, bird or butterfly in flight.)

Back drops:
interior of home
forest
cave
You can use a long strip of paper or cloth to make a backdrop that can slide across

the stage to create the different scenes.

CAVE ....FOREST ....HOUSE

Scene One

(Luba is sweeping the house. As she sweeps, she sings, hums, or whistles)

Mother: See that you get all of the crumbs! And Luba, I want you to wipe the frost off the windows!

(Natasha enters, dancing and singing. Take time with this; show her joy so the audience can contrast this with Luba, who is busy sweeping. Mother goes over to her and gives her a hug.)

Mother: Oh, I am so hungry. And what I would really like to eat is . . . hmmm . . . what I really want . . . are strawberries! Juicy, red, ripe strawberries! Luba! I want you to get me some strawberries. Go, go now. Find me some strawberries!

Luba: But Mother, it is winter. There is snow and ice outside. Strawberries grow in the summer.

Mother: You do as I say! I want you to go in the forest and pick strawberries. Now go. *(Gives her a basket. Then pushes her to the side of the stage. Shouts after her.)* And don't come back unless you have strawberries.

Scene Two

Luba: *(walks through the forest. She is shivering.)* Oh, I am so cold. Brrrr. I am brrrry cold.

(Wind sound. Other puppeteers make sound effects: lips in puckered "Oh" and/or tongue in sh-h-h position, etc.)

Luba: *(Shivering.)* Ooooh . . . *(Rubs hands together. Jumps up and down.)* I am going to freeze. Oh, dear. How will I ever go back home? I can't possibly find strawberries in the snow! *(She continues walking.)* Oh look. A cave. And it looks like there is a fire inside! *(She walks over to the cave and peers inside.)*

(Voices are heard before The Four Seasons appear.)

Winter: Who can be out on such a cold winter day?
Summer: Why, it's a little girl.
Spring: Come in, little girl.
Summer: Come, and get warm by our fire.
Winter: Come, sit by the fire, you must be freezing!
Luba: Oh, thank you.

(Four Seasons are visible as Luba enters cave. She sits down.)

Winter-Spring: Why look, she is wearing a cotton dress. Poor thing. Why are you outside, and dressed like that, on such a cold, wintry day?
Luba: My mother sent me. She wants me to bring her strawberries.
Summer-Fall: Strawberries! Why, child, it is winter. There are no strawberries growing now. Do you expect to find strawberries in the snow?
Luba: I don't know what to do. My mother gave me this basket and told me not to come back unless I have strawberries.

(The Four Seasons put their four heads together and whisper.)

Winter-Spring: Child, tell us something. Which season do you like best?
Luba: Which do I like best? *(Scratches her head, thinking.)* I'm not sure. I love summer, when the birds sing and the hills are covered with flowers. And I love fall, when the leaves turn red and gold. And I love winter, when I am all snuggled in my bed looking at the pictures Jack Frost draws on the windows. And I love spring, when the ice breaks in the lake and the birds come back. I can't tell you which season I like the best. I like them all!

(Four seasons nod and show that they are pleased.)

Summer-Fall: Child, would you please take this broom and sweep the snow from in front of the cave?

Luba: Of course. (*She takes broom and begins to sweep. As she sweeps, something red appears under the snow. She bends down to look. She picks it up. The audience sees, or at least suspects what it is before she speaks.*) Why, it is a strawberry! (*She resumes sweeping, and about a dozen strawberries appear.*)

Winter-Spring: Take them, child. Put them in your basket.

Luba: (*Picks strawberries and puts them in her basket.*) Oh, thank you. Thank you.

Winter-Spring: Now, child. we have a present for you. (*They point to two boxes that have been on the side of the stage.*) Which box would you like?

Luba: (*Points to the small box.*)

Summer-Fall: Very well, child. It is yours. Do not open it until you are home. You must go home now. Perhaps someday we will see you again.

Luba: Goodbye. Oh, thank you! Goodbye. (*Waves and runs off through forest, back to her house.*)

Scene Three

Mother: Luba! Didn't I tell you not to come back unless you brought me strawberries?

Luba: (*Lifts the cloth and shows her the strawberries.*)

Mother: (*Picks one up and looks at it. Tastes it.*) Ummm. Where did you get these? And why do you have a box? What is in it?

Luba: Oh, Mother, I found a cave in the forest. Four strange and wonderful beings were there. They told me I could have this box, but not to open the box until I was home. (*She opens it. They all look inside.*)

Mother: Oh!!!

Natasha: Why, it's gold and silver!

Mother: Natasha, do you see this! You must go to that cave. If they gave this good-for-nothing this treasure, imagine what they will give a charming little girl like you! Here, my sweetheart, put on this warm hat (*puts it on her*) and this cloak (*puts it on her*). Follow your sister's footprints in the snow and you will find the cave.

Natasha: I don't want to go. It's cold outside.

Mother: Now, my darling. You will be glad that you did. Soon you will come home with treasure!

Scene Four

Natasha: Brrr. It's cold. I don't like being outside. I want to be back home. (*Sees cave.*) Oh, there it is. And a nice fire, too. Oh, soon I'll be nice and warm sitting by the fire. (*She runs inside the cave and sits by the fire.*)

(*Natsha and the Four Seasons are sitting by the fire. There is silence.*)

Winter-Spring: Little girl, why are you outside on this cold winter day?

Natasha: My mother sent me here to get some treasure. Give it to me, so I can go back home.

(*Four Seasons put their heads together and whisper.*)

Winter-Spring: Child, tell us something. Which season do you like best?

Natasha: Which season do I like best? Hmmm . . . Ummmm . . . Hmmmm . . . Well, I know I don't like summer when the mosquitoes bite and it is so hot. Everything dies in the fall. And winter is too cold. And, it rains too much in the spring.

(*Four Seasons put their heads together and whisper.*)

Summer-Fall: Little girl, which of these boxes would you like to take home?

Natasha: Oh, I'll take the large box! (*takes it, turns and leaves cave.*)

Scene Five

Mother: (*Helps Natsha take off her hat and cloak.*) Oh, my darling. I was worried about you. Oh, how wonderful, you brought back a bigger box than your sister. Good for you! (*Opens it.*)

(*Luba, Natasha, and Mother make angry bee buzzzing sounds. Luba is on the side of the *stage and the bees do not bother her. They buzz around Natasha and the mother and then fly out the door or window.)*

(Optional: Mother and Natasha are looking one way, and so only Luba sees the Four Seasons fly by. One puppeteer can hold all four upright and move them together quickly over the top of the stage. Natasha and Mother continue to hop around and brush their bodies as if the bees are still all over them.)

Luba: (*Looks at audience.*) Soon I will be grown up. And then I will leave this home. I have the treasures in my box. I know everything is going to be all right.

Seasons: (*Might have them appear on top of the stage.*) And it was!

Winter: This is just a story.

Summer: But it is a *just* story!

TIPS ON PUPPET MANIPULATION

Before you start rehearsing with the script, play with each puppet. On the puppet stage, have each puppet demonstrate:

- walking slowly.
- walking quickly.
- showing a variety of moods with the body: happiness, anger, sorrow, timidity, arrogance, friendliness, thinking. See if the other puppeteers can guess what you are trying to convey.
- Discuss the voices. Try to create a distinctive voice for each character.

Mother Holle

Puppet Play Script for Hand and Shadow Puppets
Easily Adaptable for Overhead Projector

This can be performed by a solo puppeteer, but it is recommended for two performers.

You will need:

Two girl <u>hand</u> puppets: Use different colors for their dresses and hair ribbons. The colored hair ribbon will identify them as different characters in the shadow part of the production: you will only have to make one figure, as changing the color of the hair ribbon will identify two different girls. Fortunately, they do not have to appear on the screen at the same time.

    a slide whistle
    feathers
    well
    spindle
    Velcro
    gold streamers
    small scissors
    sign saying ACT TWO

Shadow Figures:

tree
sheep (attach heavy wool with Velcro so wool can be cut)
cow
Mother Holle
girl with add-on hair ribbon to change characters
broom
wool
apples
spindle
quilt

For directions on making shadow puppet stages and shadow puppet stages: *Worlds of Shadow: Teaching with Shadow Puppets,* David and Donna Wisniewski. (Englewood, CA: Teachers Ideas Press, 1997) $24. Phone orders: 800-237-6124. No charge for post-office shipping; add $5 for shipping by UPS. ISBN# 1-56308450-3. Appx. 200 pages.

• • •

The Puppeteers of America has a lending library of books and audio-visual aides. For information about the lending library and the puppetry festivals, guilds, consultants, and their quarterly Journal contact: P of A, c/o Gayle Schluter, 5 Crinklewood Path, Pasadena, CA 91107-1002.

Act One

(The first scene takes place in front of the shadow screen. A well is on the side of the stage, and a girl sits on the opposite end of the stage. The girl is holding a spindle, and her hand is winding around as if she is making thread.)

Girl: *(Sitting, sings, hums, or whistles. She pulls her hand up and looks at it, then shakes her head.)* Oh! Oh, my. I have cut my hand. I'll wash it in the well. *(she walks over to the well and leans over. A slide whistle sound is heard.)* Oh, no. My spindle has fallen. Mother will beat me if I go home without my spindle. What should I do? *(turns to audience.)* "Do you think I should go down the well and see if I can find it? I am so frightened. *(Looks down the well. Walks back and forth in front of it.)* I don't know what else to do. *(Climbs up on the well, and the slide whistle sound is heard again.)* I'm f-a-l-l-i-n-g.

(The light is turned on for the shadow screen. The girl is sitting in a field.)

Girl: Oh, my. *(Shakes each arm, each hand, each leg, each foot. Rolls her head around.)* I seem to be all right. I wonder where I am?

Tree: Little girl, little girl.

Girl: *(Looks the wrong way.)*

Tree: Over here.

Girl: *(Looks at tree.)*

Tree: Please help me. There are too many apples on my branches. Oh — they are so full of apples. It hurts. Would you please help me and pick some of my apples?

Girl: Of course, I will! (*Goes to tree and picks apples. Sings a song.*) Apple tree, have you seen my spindle?

Tree: No, I have not seen your spindle. Perhaps Mother Holle can help you. Thank you, little girl. Bless you.

Girl: Good-bye, tree.

Sheep: *Baaa. Baaa.* Little girl, little girl, would you please help me? My wool is so thick and heavy I can barely move. There is a scissors over there.

Girl: Of course, I will. (*Runs to get scissors and cuts [cut, or pull velcro wool off.] Use tongue click to make a scissor sound.*) Sheep, have you seen my spindle?

Sheep: *Baaa.* No, I have not seen your spindle. Perhaps Mother Holle can help you. Oh, thank you, and bless you.

Girl: Good-bye.

Cow: Little girl, little girl. Would you please milk me? There is a bucket on my horn.

Girl: Of course. (*Takes bucket from cow's horn. Milks. Makes tshh sound as she milks.*) Cow, have you seen my spindle?

Cow: No, I have not seen your spindle. Perhaps Mother Holle can help you. Oh, thank you, and bless you.

Girl: Good-bye, cow.

(*A house appears. The little girl slowly walks over and peers inside. A woman appears.*)

Mother Holle: Well, a visitor! Hello, little girl. Would you help me for a while? I need some help in my house.

Girl: Of course, I will. What do you want me to do?

Mother Holle: Can you dust and sweep and make my bed?

Girl: Of course.

Mother Holle Woman: You must be very careful with my feather quilt and shake it out just so.

Girl: I will do my best. (*Sings. Dusts, sweeps, and shakes feather quilt. A few feathers fly.*) Mother Holle, I have finished my work.

Mother Holle: So you have. And what a good job you have done! Do you want to stay with me always?

Girl: I would like to stay because you are very nice to me. But I think I had better go home. I miss my family. Do you mind?

Mother Holle: Of course not. Here is a present for you. *(sprinkles gold on her. Then she hands her her spindle.)*

Girl: Oh, thank you! *(runs down path and meets the cow.)*

Cow: Here is some cheese for you to take home.

Girl: *(Strokes cow and picks up a package of cheese.)* Thank you. *(continues and meets sheep.)*

Sheep: Here is some wool for you to take home.

Girl: *(Strokes sheep and picks up wool.)* Thank you. *(continues and meets tree.)*

Tree: Please take some apples home with you.

Girl: *(picks up apples.)* Thank you, tree.

(Shadow light is turned off, and girl puppet appears in front of screen.)

Girl: Oh, I am back! Mother! *(runs off stage.)*

Sign ACT TWO is shown to audience.
Same scene as first, but a different girl is sitting there.

Girl 2: Oh, why do I have to be here? Just because goody-goody two shoes went after her spindle doesn't mean I have to do it. But mother made me come here. She told me what to do. But I am *not* going to cut my hand! *(goes over to well and throws her spindle down. Slide whistle sound.)* Now I am supposed to go down after it. *(Shakes her head and walks away. Then goes back. Walks further away. Goes back. Leans over and looks down. Holds her nose.)* Here goes. *(Slide whistle sound.)*

(Shadow show light.)

Girl 2: Ow! Oh, I don't like this place.

Tree: Hello, little girl. Would you please pick some of my apples? My branches are hurting.

Girl 2: I don't have time.

Sheep: Hello, little girl. Would you please cut my wool? I can hardly move.

Girl 2: I don't have time.

Cow: Hello, little girl. Would you please milk me?

Girl 2: I don't have time. *(Sees house and goes over to it.)* Mother Holle, where are you? I have come to get some presents.

Mother Holle: Hello, little girl. I do need some help. Will you work for me?

Girl: N– *(Starts to say "no.")* Um–m–m . . .Sure! What do I have to do?

Mother Holle: Sweep and dust and every day shake out my feather quilt. But you must be careful how you shake my quilt. Every time the quilt shakes, it snows somewhere in the world.

Girl: Cool. *(Sweeps badly. Dusts badly. Mumbles and complains. Shakes quilt and feathers fly about.)*

Mother Holle: That is enough. It is time for you to go home.

Girl: *(In a stage whisper.)* Good! Now I will get showered with gold. *(Stands tall waiting for this to happen.)*

(Mother Holle sprinkles pitch on her. Then gives her spindle. Girl runs out. Bumps into cow. Bumps into sheep. Bumps into tree. Light goes out on shadow screen.)

Mother: *(In front of curtain, addressing audience.)* I was always angry at Grindelia, and I always thought Britt was perfect. But now I see that Grindelia is going to bring me great pride and happiness as a mother, and Britt is a lazy good-for-nothing. I may never be able to get all that pitch off of Britt. I hope she has learned a lesson. And I hope you have enjoyed this play. I would like to introduce the cast members. Cow was played by cow. *(Bring your shadow shape out in front and show it.)* Sheep was played by sheep. *(Bring sheep out.)* Tree was played by tree. *(Bring tree out.)* Mother Holle and the girls were played by *(Step out and bow.)*

(Stay in front while your audience claps. Do not leave until the applause stops!)

The Sparrow's Gift:

Matchbox Felt Board Story

You will need:
- empty *large* matchbox
- felt
- needle and thread for bird's wing
- small piece of gold foil
- glue
- Velcro (if pieces will be made of paper or cardboard)

Procedure:

1. Glue a piece of felt over the top of the matchbox to make a felt board.

2. Make the following from felt or out of paper with a piece of Velcro attached to the back:

a.   Man #1

b.   Man #2

c.   Bird (attach a thread to one wing)

d.   Two small boxes

e.   Three or four snakes

f.   Gold coins (circles cut out of foil and glued on the bottom side of the box)

The felt pieces will adhere to the felt background. If pieces are made of cardboard, glue Velcro or felt to the backs to make them stick to the felt background piece. (You can purchase precut small felt circles.)

Store pieces inside the box. This makes a handy portable felt board. When performing, leave the matchbox open so that you can easily reach the characters and boxes as you tell the story.

Announce: The Matchbox Theater presents *The Sparrow's Gift*, a folktale from Japan.

1. *(Put one man and the bird on the box.)* Oh, you poor little bird. Did you fall from that tree? You are hurt. I will take care of you. *(Pretend to feed the bird. Stroke it.)* You are getting better. Soon you will be able to fly. *(Pretend to feed the bird. Stroke it so it seems like some time has passed. Then pick up the piece of thread from the top wing and make the wing flap.)* Oh, little bird, your wing is better. You can fly. Goodbye, little bird.

2. *(Take the man and bird off. Then put the bird back and add the two boxes.)*

3. *(Bring the man back.)* You want to thank me? You want me to choose one of these boxes? Well, then, I will take the smaller one. Thank you, little bird.

4. *(Take the bird and the large box away.)*

5. *(Pretend to peek under the small box.)* Oh, my! Gold! How wonderful!

6. *(Take everything off. Put the second man on.)* My neighbor got a lot of gold from a bird he took care of as a reward. I want gold, too. I know what I will do. I will throw a stone at the next bird I see, and then I will take care of it. When it is better, it will reward me with gold.

7. *(Bring the bird back)* Man whispers: Oh, I hit it with the stone! Now, little bird I will take care of you, and you can give me gold! *(In a louder voice, to the bird.)* I will take care of you, bird. There. You are getting better already. Oh, look, now you can fly. *(Pull the string.)*

8. *(Take the bird away and bring it back with the two boxes.)* You want me to choose one of the boxes for my reward? I will take the large one!

9. *(Take the bird away.)*

10. Now I will have even more gold than my neighbor! *(Pretend to look under the box.)* Oh, no! Oh, dear! Snakes! It's not fair! I took care of that bird. It's not fair. Not fair at all.

11. *(Take this man and his box away.)*

12. *If you want, put up a little sign: "The End." Or you might want to say:* This is just a story. But it is a *just* story.

Additional Story Scripts

For Puppets

"The Old Woman of the West," in L. Olfson, *You Can Put on a Show* (1975). Brothers as main characters. Improvisational ending, asking audience if the evil brother deserves to be punished. No royalty.

Lewis Mahlman and David C. Jones, "Toads and Diamonds," in *Folktale Plays for Puppets*. (Boston: Plays, 1980).

For Actors

Ernestine Phillips, "Aesop — Man of Fables," in Sylvia E. Kamerman, ed., *Fifty Plays for Junior Actors* (Boston: Plays, 1966). Eight characters. No royalty.

Hazel W. Corson, "Dame Fortune and Don Money," in Sylvia E. Kamerman, ed., *Dramatized Folktales of the World: A Collection of Fifty One Act Plays*. (Boston: Plays, 1971). Thirteen characters. No royalty. Asks the question, "Which brings happiness? Luck or money?"

Loretta Camp Capwell, "Tongue-Cut Sparrow," in Sylvia E. Kamerman, ed., *Children's Plays from Favorite Stories* (Boston: Plays, 1978). Seventeen characters. No royalty.

Barbara Winther, "Macona the Honest Warrior," in *Plays: The Drama Magazine for Young People* (Feb. 1978), pp. 52–57. South American tale. Seven characters. No royalty.

Jean Feather, "One Wish Too Many," in Sylvia E. Kamerman, ed., *Plays from Favorite Folk Tales* (Boston: Plays, 1987). Baucis and Philemon story in a contemporary setting.

"The Widow and the Wealthy Neighbor," in Kim Alan Wheetley, *"Tales of Trickery: A Triad of Comic Indonesian Tales"* (Chicago: Dramatic Publishing Co., 1981).

"Theater for a Small Planet," in Jules Tasca, *Theater for a Small Planet* (Venice, Fla.: Eldridge Publishers, 1992).

Janet Brown, "The Lake at the End of the World," in *Plays: The Drama Magazine for Young People* (Boston: Plays, March 1993), pp. 39–48. An Inca legend.

Jamie Turner, "The White Spider's Gift," in *Plays: The Drama Magazine for Young People* (March 1990), pp. 31–38. A folk tale from Paraguay.

S. Marshak, *Twelve Months: A Fairy Tale* (Moscow: Foreign Languages Publishing House, 1967). Twenty-six characters. This delightful adaptation has a stubborn, ill-mannered princess and a kind soldier, as well as the kind and unkind stepsisters. It includes long speeches but could easily be adapted.

Classroom Word Game:
Kind and Unkind

A spelling game using the concept of opposites for two teams of twelve players

You will need:
- 24 pieces of paper, each to have a letter written on it in large print
- safety pins to attach the letters to the backs of the 24 students

Procedure:
1. Make two sets of the twelve letters A, D, E, H, I, L, N, O, R, T, W, Y. Use a different colored felt pen for each team.
2. Pin a letter on the back of each player.
3. Have the teams line up on opposite sides of the room facing each other.
4. Call out a word. Team members decide on a word meaning the *opposite* of the word called out. Team members with the letters in that word spell out the word and stand with their backs facing the center of the room so that the teacher can read the word.
5. The first team to have a word, the opposite of the word called out, spelled correctly, gets a point.

Following is a list of words to be used. Call out the words in capital letters. Students need to spell the words in parentheses. Note that students may think of other words that are the opposite of the word the teacher calls out, but they must be able to spell the word with the letters available to them.

Simple Words

YOUNG (old)
PEACE (war)
NIGHT (day)
NARROW (wide)
WET (dry)
UP (down)
SOUTH (north)
BLACK (white)
CATCH (throw)
SOFT (hard)
COLD (hot)
CLEAN (dirty)
LOVE (hate)
TAIL (head)
YES (no)
WALK (ride) or (run)
NIGHT (day)
OFF (on)
DRY (wet)
ENORMOUS (tiny)
LATE (early)
LASS (lad)
FOLLOW (lead)
FAT (thin)
LIVE (die)
LENGTH (width)
LOSE (win)
SUMMER (winter)
EARLY (late)
HEAD (tail)
FAR (near)
FIND (hide)
TRUTH (lie)

A little harder:

BORROW (loan)
THEN (now)
ENERGETIC (tired)
DIVORCE (wed)
GOOD-BYE (hi)
FIRE (hire) or (water)
COOKED (raw)
YANG (yin)
INCOMPLETE (whole)
LAND (water)
NOW (wait) or (later)
FAST (eat) or (dine)

VIII
CHARTS

(I) COUNTRIES FROM WHICH TEXTS WERE OBTAINED

Country	Full Text	Summary	Citation
Africa	12,13,14,16	34,53,54,55	
Albania	5		
American Indian	25,27,30	52	
Austria		35	
Brazil			57
Brittany	15	36	
Burma			58
Chili		37	
China		38	65,66,67
England	20,21	39	
Eskimo		40	
Ethiopia	69		
France	24		
Germany	6,7		
Greece	1,2,3	51	
Haiti		41	
Iceland	31		
India	10,11		
Iran		42	
Ireland	18,19,33		
Italy	26,28	43, 44,55	
Japan	8	45,46,47,48,56	59,60,61
Korea			69,70
Micronesia	9		
Norway	22		
Poland			71
Portugal		49	
Scotland		50	
Spain	32		62
Russia	4,29		
United States	17,23		63,64,72

(II) PROTAGONISTS

Although Tale Type 480 is referred to as "The Kind and Unkind Girl," the main characters are often neighbors, brothers, grown women and men, or even animals.

NAME OF STORY AND COUNTRY	STORY NUMBER

(1) Sisters

Peesie and Beansie (India)	10
Humility Rewarded (India)	11
Three Girls and Journey-Cake (USA)	17
Corpse Watchers (Ireland)	18
Old Hag's Long Leather Bag (Ireland)	19
Green Lady (England)	21
House of Cats (Italy)	26
Juanita, Marianeta, the Cat and the Bear (Am. Indian)	30
Servant at the Fairy's (Spain)	32
Gallymanders (USA)	64
Girl and the Dead Man (Scotland)	50
Old Witch (England)	39
Moon Pearls (Iran)	42
Snake Chief (Africa)	34
The Bucket (Italy)	28

(2) Stepsisters

Twelve Months (Greece)	3
King Frost (Russia)	4
Three Little Men (Germany)	6
Mother Holle (Germany)	7
Black of Heart (Africa)	12
Three Heads of the Well (England)	20
Two Step Sisters (Norway)	22
Blindman's Bluff (Russia)	29
Three Mermaids (Ireland)	36
Toads and Diamonds (France)	24
Tale of the Cats (Italy)	44
Water in the Basket (Italy)	43
Hearth Cat (Portugal)	49
Story of Spiola (Am. Indian)	52

APPENDIX ONE

Animals mentioned in these stories

Bear
Juanita, Marianeta
Blindman's Bluff

Bees
The Sparrow's Gifts

Bird
The Sparrow's Gift
The Three Girls and the Journey Cake
The Two Step Sisters
The Man Who Cuts Down the Cinnamon tree

Buffalo
Peesie and Beansie

Camel
Black of Heart

Cat
Juanita, Marianeta
House of Cats
Mother of the Waters (s)
Colony of Cats (s)
The Corpse Watchers
Moon Pearls (s)

Chicken
The Talking Eggs
The Tale of the Cats (s)

Centipedes
The Sparrow's Gift (s)

Cow/Cattle
Old Hag and Leather Bag
Two Step Sisters
Black of Heart
The Old Witch (s)
The Hearth Cat (s)

Dog
King Frost
Black of Heart
Blindman's Bluff
The Servant at the Fairies
Old Man of the Flowers (s)
The Girl and the Dead Man (s)
The Corpse Watchers

Donkey
House of Cats
Servant at the Fairies
Two Brothers
Good Child and the Bad
Water in the Basket (s)

Fish

The Twelve Months

The Two Brothers

Two Brothers and ther Enmity

The Good Child and the Bad

The Green Lady

Frog

Two Step Sisters

The Girl and the Hogs

Snake Chief

Goat

The Old Hag's Long Leather Bag

Snake Chief

Hen

Rooster and Hen

Hog

Girl and the Hogs

Horse

King Frost

The Sparrow's Gift

Humility rewarded

House of Cats

The Old Hag's Long Leather Bag

Black of Heart

Horsefly

The Sparrow's Gift

Jackal

String of Beads

Lizard

Mother of the Waters (s)

The Sparrow's gifts

Mouse

Snake Chief

Blindman's Bluff

The Rolling Rice Ball

Ostrich

Black of Heart

Partridge

Black of Heart

Rooster

Mother Holle

Rooster and Hen

The Man Who Cut Down the
Cinnamon tree (s)

Scorpion

The Sparrow's Gifts

Sheep

Old Hag's Long Leather Bag

Two Step Sisters

Black of Heart

Snake
    Rooster and Hen
    Humility rewarded
    Anansi
    Two Step Sisters
    The Sparrow's Gift
    The Snake Chief
    Talking Eggs
    Diamond and Toads
    Twelve Months
    Corpse Watchers
    Two Stepsisters

Toad
    Toads and Diamonds
    Two Step Sisters

Wasps
    The Sparrow's Gifts (s)

Whale
    The Two Rich Girls (s)

Worms
    Colony of Cats (s)

(s) = summarized texts

APPENDIX TWO:

Foods mentioned in these stories

Apples
Two Step Sisters
Mother Holle
Corpse Watcher
The Old Witch

Banana Pudding
Mother of the Waters

Beans
Mother of the Waters
Colony of Cats
Miraculous Pitcher

Bread
Miraculous Pitcher
Three Little Men
Girl and Hogs
Old Witch
Mother Holle
Old Hag and Leather Bag
Twelve Months
How the Good Gifts were Used by
Two
Three Heads in the Well

Breadfruit
The Girl Who Gave Breadfuit

Butter
Three Little Men
Two Step Sisters

Cabbages
Miraculous Pitcher

Cakes
Three Little Men
Three Girls with Journey
Green Lady
Tale of the Cats
Copse Watchers
Black of Heart
Peesie and Beansie
The Rolling Rice Ball

Cauliflower
Colony of Cats

Cheese
The Miraculous Pitcher
The Three Heads in the Well

Chicory
Colony of Cats

Corn
House of Cats

Cheese
Miraculous Pitcher
Three Heads of the Well

Chicken (roasted)
The Tale of the Cats

Eggs
Rooster and Hen
Talking Eggs
The Brothers and the Eggs
Mother of the Waters

Fish
Two Brothers and Their Enmity
The Green Lady
Twelve Months

Macaroni
The Tale of the Cats

Meat
Tale of the Cats
Juanita, Marianeta

Milk
Old Witch
Humility rewarded
Two Step Sisters
Snake Chief
Miraculous Pitcher

Onions
Miraculous Pitcher

Onion leaves
Making Stew

Orange
The Perfect Orange

Pancakes
King Frost

Peas
Miraculous Pitcher

Pepper
Making Stew

Plums
Peesie and Beansie

Porridge
Black of Heart
Blindman's Bluff

Pumpkin
The Man Who Cut Down the Cinnamon Tree

Rice
The Sparrow's Gift
Humility Rewarded
Talking Eggs
Mother of Waters
Black of Heart
The Rolling Rice Ball

Salt
Making Stew

Sausage
Tale of the Cats
The Four Little Dwarfs

Soup
Black of Heart
Anansi

Spice
Making Stew

Stew
Black of Heart
Making Stew
Juanita, Marianeta, the Cat and the
    Bear

Strawberries
Three Little Men in the Woods
Story of Spiola

Sugar cane
Two Brothers and their Enmity

Vegetables
Anansi
The Sparrow's Gifts
House of Cats

Vinegar
Colony of Cats

PERMISSIONS, ACKNOWLEDGMENTS, AND STORY SOURCES

The Golden Axe (Greece)
This story is usually titled "Mercury and the Workmen" in collections of Aesop Fables.

The Miraculous Pitcher (Greece)
This story developed through oral retellings by Ruth Stotter. It is included in numerous collections of Greek folk tales and originated in *The Metamorphoses,* by the Roman poet Ovid, who lived 43 B.C..

The Twelve Months (Greece)
This story developed through oral retellings by Ruth Stotter. "The Twelve Months" appears in numerous collections, including *Modern Greek Folktales,* by R. M. Dawkins (London: Oxford Publishers, 1953); *Folktales of Greece,* by Georgios A. Megas, trans. Helen Colaclides (Chicago: University of Chicago Press, 1970), pp. 123-127; *Greek Fairy Tales,* by Barbara Kerr Wilson (New York and Chicago: Follett Publishers, 1966), pp. 225-230; *Favorite Fairy Tales Told Around the World,* retold by Virginia Haviland (Boston: Little, Brown, 1985).

King Frost (Russia)
"The Story of King Frost," in Andrew Lang, ed., *The Yellow Fairy Book* (New York: Dover Publications, 1966; originally London: Longmans, Green and Co., 1894), pp. 209-212.

The Rooster and the Hen (Albania)
"The Rooster and the Hen," in *Tricks of Women and Other Albanian Tales,* trans. Paul Fennimore Cooper (N.Y.: Wm. Morrow & Co., 1928), pp. 87-88.

The Three Little Men in the Woods (Germany)
"The Three Dwarfs," in Andrew Lang, ed., *The Red Fairy Book* (New York: Dover Publications,1966; originally London: Longmans, Green and Co., 1890), pp. 238-245.

Mother Holle (Germany)
"Mother Holle," in Andrew Lang, ed., *The Red Fairy Book* (New York: Dover Publications, 1966; originally London: Longmans, Green and Co., 1890), pp. 303-306.

The Sparrow's Gift (Japan)
"The Sparrow's Gift" in Keigo Seki, ed. *Folktales of Japan*, trans. Robert J. Adams (Chicago: University of Chicago, 1963). Printed by permission of University of Chicago. No further reproduction is permitted.

The Two Brothers (Micronesia)
"The Two Brothers," in Eve Grey, *Legends of Micronesia, Book Two*. Published by the High Commissioner, Trust territory of the Pacific Islands, Department of Education, 1951, pp. 76-80.

Peesie and Beansie (Panjib and Kashmir, India)
"Peesie and Beansie," in F.A. Steele and R. C. Temple, *Wide Awake Stories* (Bombay, India: Education Society's Press, 1884) pp. 178-183.

Humility Rewarded and Pride Punished (Bengal, India)
"Humility Rewarded and Pride Punished," in F. B. Bradley-Birt, *Bengal Fairy Tales,* ill. Abanindranath Tague (New York: Jon Lane Co., 1920) pp. 191-195.

Black of Heart (Hausa, Africa)
"The Orphans," adapted from R. S. Rattray, *Hausa Folk-Lore, Customs, Proverbs, etc.* (1913; reissued 1969), pp. 130-160. By permission of Oxford University Press. No further reproduction is permitted.

Making Stew (Hausa, Africa)
"Salt, Sauce and Onion Leaves," adapted from R. S. Rattray, *Hausa Folk-Lore, Customs, Proverbs, etc.* (1913; reissued 1969), pp. 260-272. By permission of Oxford University Press. No further reproduction is permitted.

The String of Beads (Congo, Africa)
"The String of Beads," from May Augustine Klippie, *African Folk Tales with Foreign Analogues (*Muncie, Ind.: Ball State Teacher's College, Department of English, 1938), pp. 366-368. Ph.D. thesis (microfilm).

The Gift of the Mermaid (Celtic, Brittany)

"The Gift of the Mermaid," Story abstract summarized from *Les Litte'ratures Populaires de Toutes Les Nations, Tome XXV: Contes Populaire de Base-Bretagne*, par F.M. Luzel, Tome II. G.P. Maisonneuve & Larose, ed. (Paris 1967); oral telling by storyteller John Boe (Berkeley, California); *The Gift of The Mermaid in Celtic Folk and Fairy Tales*, ed. and adapted by Eric and Nancy Protter (New York: Duell, Sloan and Pearce, 1966), pp. 142-146.

Anansi and His Son (Ashanti, Africa)

"Pot and Whip: Why There are Remedies for Snake Bites," in Melville Herskovits and Francis S. Herskovits, *Tales in Pidgin English from Ashanti*. Reproduced by permission from the Journal of American Folklore, vol. 50, ed. by Ruth Benedict (1937), pp. 73-75.

The Three Girls and the Journey-Cakes (Appalachia, United States)

"The Three Girls and the Journey Cakes," in Marie Campbell, *Tales from the Cloud Walking Country* (1958), pp. 140-143. Permission to use this story granted from Indiana University Press. No further reproduction is permitted.

The Corpse Watchers (Wexford, Ireland)

"Corpse Watchers," in Patrick Kennedy, *Legendary Fictions of the Irish Celts* (London, 1866), pp. 54-77. Also in Henry Glassie, *Irish Tales* (New York: Pantheon Books, 1985), pp. 263-266.

The Old Hag's Long Leather Bag (Ireland)

"The Old Hag's Long Leather Bag," in *Donegal Fairy Tales,* collected and told by Seumas MacManus (Dover Publications, 1968; originally published by McClure, Phillips and Co., 1909).

The Three Heads of the Well (England)

"The Three Heads of the Well," in Joseph Jacobs, *English Folk and Fairy Tales* (New York: Putman, n.d.), pp. 222-227.

The Green Lady (England)

"The Green Lady," in Katharine M. Briggs and Ruth L. Tongue, ed., *Folktales of England* (1965), pp. 6-10. Permission to use this story from the University of Chicago Press. No further reproduction is permitted.

The Two Stepsisters (Norway)
"The Two Step-Sisters," in *East O' the Sun and West O' the Moon* (New York: Dover Publications, 1970). This story was collected by Peter Christen Asbjornsen and Jorgen E. Moe and appears in *Norwegian Folk Tales*.

The Talking Eggs (Creole, United States)
From *Memoirs of the American Folklore Society*. This story can also be found in *Danny Kayes Around the World Story Book* (New York: Random House, 1960.)

Diamonds and Toads (France)
"Toads and Diamonds," in the Charles Perrault collection of tales, reprinted in Andrew Lang, ed., *The Blue Fairy Book* (New York: Dover Publications, 1965; originally London: Longmans, Green and Co., ca 1889), pp. 274-277.

The Girls and the Hogs (Mushkogean, America Indian)
"The Girls and the Hogs," in John R. Swanton, *Indians of the Mushkogean Stock, Alabama and Kosati Tribes*. Journal of American Folklore, Vol. 26 (1912-1913), p. 211.

House of Cats (Italy)
"The House of the Cats," in Andrew Lang, ed., *The Crimson Fairy Book* (New York: Dover, 1967; originally London: Longmans, Green and Co., 1903), pp. 340-49

The Good Child and the Bad (Spanish tale from Zuni, Southwest American Indian)
"The Good Child and the Bad," in E. C. Parsons and F. Boas, *Spanish Tales from Laguna and Zuni, Journal of American Folklore* 33 (1920), 71-72.

The Bucket (Milan, Italy)
"The Bucket," in Thomas Frederick Crane, A. M., *Italian Popular Tales* (London: Houghton Mifflin, 1885), pp. 100-102.

Blindman's Bluff (Russia)
Story summarized from "Daughter and Stepdaughter" in Janet Higgonnet Schnopper, *Tales from Atop a Russian Stove* (Chicago: Albert Whitman and Co., 1973), pp. 109-117; "Daughter and Step Daughter" in Aleksandr Afanas'ev *Russian Fairy Tales*; "Baba Yaga," in many Russian story collections.

Juanita, Marianeta, the Cat, and the Bear (San Juan Pueblo, American Indian)

"Juanita, Marianeta, the Cat and the Bear," in *Taytay's Tales,* collected and retold by Elizabeth DeHuff. (New York: Harcourt, Brace & Co., 1922) pp. 8-13.

The Blind Beggar (Iceland)

"Playing Blind Beggar," in *Icelandic Folktales and Legends.* Copyright (c) 1972 Jacqueline Simpson. Permission to use this story from the University of California. No further reproduction is permitted.

The Servant at the Fairies (Basque, Spain)

"The Servant at the Fairies," in M. Julian Vinson, *Basque Legends* (London: Griffith and Farran, 1877).

The Legend of Knockgrafton (Ireland)

"The Legend of Knockgrafton," in Joseph Jacobs *More Celtic Tales* (New York: Dover Publications, 1968; originally David Nutt, 1894), 156-163. Also called "The Hunchback's Gift," Tale 38 in Stith Thompson, *One Hundred Favorite Folktales.*

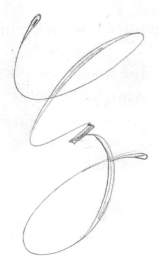